The Soul of Lyskerrys

Robert Beck

First published in Great Britain by Mandolin Press 2019

MANDOLIN PRESS

Copyright © 2019 Robert Beck

The right of Robert Beck to be identified as the author of the work has been asserted by him in accordance with the Copyright, Designs and Patents Act 1988

Printed by TJ International Ltd, Padstow, Cornwall.

Editing by Dream Edit Repeat

www.dreameditrepeat.com

Cover design by Spiffing Covers

www.spiffingcovers.com

ISBN-13: 978-0-9956734-3-4

www.robertbeckauthor.com

DEDICATION

For Paula.

ACKNOWLEDGMENTS

If you enjoy this book, then you have my editor, Ashley Wyrick, to thank for it. While I stumbled through the Otherworld, totally beguiled, simply writing everything I saw, Ashley guided me through to the finished story. The Soul of Lyskerrys would be a much poorer tale without her insight and dedication.

Thanks are also in order for my valued beta readers: Jess Hoggett and Hannah Cartwright. Jess, for blasting through an eleventh-hour manuscript and returning a brilliantly comprehensive critique in almost no time at all. And Hannah, for offering to help after a chance meeting caused by a cancelled train through Cornwall. I also would like to thank Debs Pick and Melanie Kimpton for reading through early revisions of The Soul of Lyskerrys back when it was still called The Ghost of Lyskerrys. Insights into Jacob's character were provided by various computer gamers of my acquaintance, without whom I would never have learned what a rage-quit was.

There are many others of course, and if I forgot to mention anyone then I'm sorry.

Finally, I want to thank my wife, Paula, and our sons, Lewis, Elliot, and Thomas. Between them, they have put up with a lot of deranged rambling about places they have never seen and have endured more than their fair share of sales events. You're the best!

Robert Beck. Liskeard/Lyskerrys 2019

PROLOGUE

No one could survive a fall from this height. You'd have what, three seconds? Four at the most. The man peered over the edge of the waterfall and counted. Four seconds - maximum - then it'd be Game Over.

Looking down had been a mistake. His new perspective caused the world around him to sway sickeningly.

Even in the darkness of the early hours, he could sense the unstoppable power of the water as the river plunged over the precipice. He could hear it in the tremendous roar that blocked out all other sound, feel it in the vibrations rumbling up through his feet, and taste it in the spray of mist against his face.

Curving smoothly over the edge of the falls, the water seemed unaware that anything had changed, and for a few moments it continued trying to be a river. But soon enough gravity took hold, tearing it apart and remaking it into a churning, unstoppable torrent, before slamming it into the rocks far below.

The man shuddered. If it tried the same thing with him, he would split open like a piece of overripe fruit, his vital, secret biology exposed to the uncaring night air in a spray of crimson.

A splash of cold water soaked through his shoes. He ignored it. Given his current situation, it hardly mattered. Instead he carefully lifted his gaze towards the stars.

Swallowing, the man blinked away a sudden swell of emotion. No matter how many times he looked at the night sky here, he would never become accustomed to it. Arching above him, fragile veils of dust twisted and rippled through the void. Distant supernovae blossomed before his eyes and died in an instant. The stars were astonishingly bright and shone with a purity that illuminated the dark places in the man's soul.

Reminded of his insignificance in the unimaginable enormity of the cosmos, he returned his attention to the present moment. Thick glassy ropes of water slid past reflecting the hard, cold light of the stars. To either side, rocks, like the one on which he stood, protruded from the surface of the water like crenellations on a drowned castle. Each one green and slick with algae.

The horizon tilted again, and the man staggered a step to the side, as another nauseating wave of vertigo broke over him.

But all was not as futile as it appeared, because the man teetering on the edge of the world knew a secret.

Forcing himself to take deep calming breaths, and keeping his attention locked on the horizon, he patted at his jacket pocket. A reassuring solidness, the reason he was here in the first place, met his touch. The weight of the stone briefly returned the man's thoughts to his dangerous journey along the lip of the waterfall to reach this precarious position.

A chill ran across his back. Was that movement – out there, in the dark across the water? Was it possible he wasn't alone out here? The man twisted around carefully, looking back over his shoulder. Could he have been followed? But as hard as he tried to focus on the thought, it seemed intent on eluding him. Anyway, what did it matter if anyone had seen him? There was only one way he was getting out of this situation. Let them follow him.

He slipped his hand into his pocket and closed his fingers around what lay within. Withdrawing it, he gazed adoringly downward and sighed as a feeling of utter contentment flowed through him. The jewel loved him. He had stolen it from where it had laid, for thousands of years for all he knew, and yet still it loved him.

Had there been anyone else present to observe the thief at that time, they would have seen him close his eyes and smile, his face bathed in the aquamarine glow drifting languidly from the gemstone.

Then they would have seen him step off the edge of the world and plunge into the abyss.

CHAPTER 1

The face of the woman, who had just run her finger somewhat seductively across Jacob Trevorrow's cheek, dissolved away and was replaced by the harsh glare of a sodium lamp. Jacob struggled to make sense of this bizarre transition as he gradually surfaced nearer to wakefulness. The soft caress he'd been enjoying resolved into a rivulet of cold water running down the side of his face.

Jacob closed his eyes again and curled into a tighter ball. Just a few more minutes, then he'd wake up and deal with whatever was happening. He was still close enough to sleep to believe this could all be solved by simply returning to the delicious world of his dreams: a world where he was warm instead of shivering; where his back didn't ache; and, most importantly at the moment, a world in which his pillow didn't feel like a rock.

But it was already too late. Rationality was seeping through his mind like water through worn shoes, asking inconvenient questions about why his clothes felt damp and pointing out that simply going back to sleep wouldn't actually change anything.

Scowling, Jacob half opened one eye. The flat, starless sky reflected the yellow glow of the lamp on the top of Liskeard's fountain. The fountain - what a bloody joke - a dull monument to some engineer, nothing more than a drinking fountain. The whole scene was tipped over onto its side.

Granite pressed hard into the side of his head, and reluctantly he raised himself up onto one arm. His chilled muscles protested at the movement. The fountain rotated into its more usual orientation, and Jacob shivered as night air flowed into his lungs, unexpectedly cold and fresh. Shit - he'd been sleeping on the ground in the centre of town again, and for quite some time by the feel of things.

Staggering to his feet, Jacob grasped the edge of the fountain for support. The act of standing up brought new areas of clothing, not warmed by his body heat, into contact with his skin; the night's rain had soaked him through. Still, at least he was dressed, which was an improvement on the last time this had happened.

As full consciousness returned, new worries clamoured for attention. He'd obviously been sleepwalking again. What if someone had seen him? How long had he been out here? Had he locked the door? Had he even closed it?

Fucking great. His family were already regarded as freaks, thanks to his dad banging on about Liskeard being a gateway to another world - this was all he needed.

Jacob turned in unsteady circles. The town was eerily quiet and empty. A glance across the road towards Pike Street, dropping away opposite him, allowed a good view of the illuminated clock face on the Guildhall tower. Three thirty in the morning - that was good - not much chance of anyone being around at this time. He shouldn't attract too much attention, not now he was up off the ground, and especially since he was fully clothed.

Shivering, Jacob folded his arms tightly across his chest and tucked his hands under his armpits. Christ it was cold!

How long had he been lying under the fountain? A double espresso, and a particularly intense game of Call of Duty, had made it a late night. It had been at least one o'clock. So... what? A couple of hours?

Okay, damage limitation time. The quickest route back to the flat was... straight across the road, down the hill and then right along Fore Street. Jacob moved out into the road.

Shit! Movement! There, at the far end of the road. Who the hell was that? Dropping to his haunches behind a granite flower planter, Jacob squinted into the distance. A relieved smile spread over his face as the rush of adrenaline faded. He'd be safe enough, just so long as he kept out of sight.

It was only the Queen of England.

CHAPTER 2

Afterwards, Peter Trevorrow would wonder why he hadn't been more unsettled by the strange and, in retrospect, rather disturbing events that were to occur that evening, but the only ominous thing about the morning had been the sound of heavy rain lashing against the bedroom window. Parting the curtains a crack, so as not to wake Catherine, he peered out at the farm cowering beneath swollen, black clouds.

After a miserable day labouring in the sodden fields, wishing he was somewhere — anywhere — else, Peter returned home in the late afternoon. leaving just enough time for a quick shower before he had to head out again for his shift at the pub. The income from the farm was never going to be enough to support a wife and two children.

As it turned out, he didn't mind working at the pub. It was a quiet sort of place, there was rarely any trouble, and every now and then a band would be booked to play which made the evening more interesting. There was no band playing that night though. In fact, there wasn't really much of anything going on, the rain had taken care of that. Peter couldn't blame his customers for staying at home; if it hadn't been for work, he wouldn't have gone out either.

By nine-thirty the bar was empty, and Peter was alone. Well, alone if you didn't count the man in the hooded sweatshirt, and his presence was odd in itself. Peter couldn't recall him coming in, and with so few customers tonight he was fairly sure he would have noticed. And, now he came to think of it, the corner of the room he was occupying wasn't usually in shadow either, a bulb must have blown. Still, the firelight from the hearth did make it look rather inviting. Perhaps that was why the stranger had chosen to sit there.

How long the man had been there? Long enough to suggest he consider buying a drink? That was what customers in pubs generally did, wasn't it? Summoning up his best barman's voice, Peter leaned forward, placed both hands firmly on the bar, and then blinked in surprise. The table in the corner was empty. Peter shook his head and blinked again. The man in the hoodie was now standing on the other side of the bar. Weird, admittedly, but at least it was one awkward conversation Peter no longer had to worry about.

Now that he was out of the shadows, Peter could see that the man wasn't wearing a sweatshirt after all. It was more like a hooded cape — the sort of thing a highwayman would wear, or an elf from one of those video games his son was always playing.

Did you even still get highwaymen? There probably wasn't much call for them these days what with motorways and fast cars and such. By the time the shout of *stand and deliver* had gone out any car would be little more than a memory. Peter rubbed his eyes with the back of his hand; his mind was wandering, and his eyelids were starting to droop. These long workdays must be getting to him. And as for elves, everyone knew there were no such things.

"Care to join me for a drink?" said the man in the cape. Bizarrely, his words were a deep shade of indigo, and mostly soft curves but with hidden barbs that would bite deeply and hold before you even noticed.

"Sorry," said Peter, "I'm feeling a bit strange all of a sudden. What did you say?" The man smiled. Did his eyes just flash orange? Orange wasn't a normal eye colour was it? Perhaps it was.

The man lowered his hood and leaned in close across the bar. "I said that you look like you could use a drink."

The man had a point. Peter was pretty sure he did need a drink, although for some strange reason he felt as though he should have been the one asking the question. He smiled at the thought, he had no idea where it had come from, surely the man must know what he was doing.

"Yeah," Peter said, "you're not wrong."

"Glass?"

Peter blinked and shook his head to clear it, his mind had been drifting again. He focussed on the man on the other side of the bar. Those pointed ears certainly suited him; you don't see ears like that too often. In fact, Peter wasn't sure he'd ever seen any quite like those. The intricate line of silver tracing the upward sweep and extenuating the tip must be some kind of jewellery, although he couldn't see how it was attached. And those odd tattoos curving across his cheekbones, that was some high-quality ink-work. Must be some new kind of dye to change hue like that with each word he spoke.

"Sorry, what?" said Peter.

"You will need a glass. Only a small one."

"Oh yes, of course." Peter reached down below the bar, found two shot-glasses and placed them onto the counter. From somewhere within his cape, the man produced an engraved silver flask and unscrewed the lid.

"Go easy with this my friend, 'tis powerful stuff." He leaned even closer to Peter and decanted a dark ruby liquid into each of the glasses. Gazing into it, Peter was reminded of documentaries he had seen of life in the deep oceans; all alluring, glassy iridescence, and lethal, needle-sharp teeth. A chill crawled across his back. Peter shuddered and snatched his gaze away from the drinks.

The man in the cloak stared intently at him, and without breaking eye contact he lifted one of the glasses and consumed the contents in a single swallow, daring Peter to do the same. The man smiled, and Peter was struck by his fine features: perfect white teeth; high, sharp cheekbones; flawless skin and those startling orange eyes. Peter was starting to feel a little uncomfortable. Mentally retreating from his unexpected distractions, he picked up his glass and drank. The man was right about one thing; the drink was very strong.

The rest of the evening proved even more difficult to maintain contact with than the first half. Peter was dimly aware of flickering firelight, drinking more of the dark liquid and of listening to the man's musical voice. Oddly, when he thought back on the events of the evening later, these vague memories were interspersed with flashes of moonlit forest tracks, of moving at a graceful run through the night between dark stands of trees, of dancing along branches high above the ground and of drifting ribbons of fireflies.

At the end of the evening, Peter had reached for his wallet to pay the man only to be reminded that he should be the one receiving payment. That was right wasn't it? The man in the cape produced a coin and clicked it down onto the bar. Peter staggered sideways, grabbing hold of the counter for support, as the pub rotated back into place around the coin. It was as if he'd had been looking at the world from slightly the wrong angle all evening, and all he needed was that one familiar sound to re-orientate himself.

When he looked up again the man was gone. In all probability he'd never really been there at all. Peter reached down to slide the coin off the bar, his fingers brushing across the illegible markings that might have once been words. That was the point when everything changed.

Suddenly Peter was aware of a connection between this world and, well, somewhere else. He couldn't see as such, but it blazed in his mind like a guiding star, and he knew where it was. Right now, it was in a secluded dell somewhere outside the nearby village of St. Keyne. There was no way he'd have time to get there and back during the working day tomorrow; any investigation would have to wait.

Over the course of the next few days Peter found that although the location of the gateway, as it seemed most convenient to think of it, wasn't always in his mind, he could summon it at will. He also noticed, that while there was only ever a single gateway, it couldn't be relied on to stay in the same place. Rather frustratingly it relocated frequently enough that he was never able to find enough time to reach it before it moved on.

For the remainder of the following week, Peter followed his evening routine of waiting for the regulars to drift off to their homes, before collecting his car, and driving back to the farm. He didn't do that on the Friday. Instead, he walked the short distance through the town to the Pipe Well, which for the preceding ten minutes had been the location of the gateway.

Of course, that had been years ago. His children were grown now, Jacob even had a full-time job, and Catherine… well, Catherine was long gone.

CHAPTER 3

She was not the real Queen of England of course but that was how everyone knew her. It was a name given to her partly because no one seemed to know her real one, but mostly because of the way she spoke. Although what she said rarely made sense, she delivered each word with perfect pronunciation, and she always referred to herself as *we*, never *I*. The Royal *we*, everyone said.

Everything the Queen of England owned, she pushed ahead of her in an old supermarket trolley. If the townsfolk didn't heed the approaching clatter, the sight of her determined blue eyes peering over a mound of carrier bags was enough to cause them to quickly move aside. And although no one could say with certainty when she had arrived, everyone agreed that the Queen had been sleeping on the streets of Liskeard for a long time.

Jacob peered nervously out from behind the raised flower planter and along the darkened street. The Queen was getting closer. As far he knew, no one had spotted him sleeping under the fountain, but if the Queen saw him the game would be up. She'd start shrieking and crying, and that'd be the end of any hope he had of sneaking home unnoticed.

He needed to get out of sight. A covered walkway between two shops looked like the nearest available hiding place. Light from the fountain slanted across the entrance, but inside looked dark enough to keep him hidden. Jacob ducked into the shadows. With luck she'd stay on the other side of the road, but he couldn't be too careful; she did have a fondness for the fountain.

A crash echoed between the shop fronts as the Queen pushed her trolley off the kerb. Damn, she was heading straight for him. The only cover in the alley was a pile of refuse sacks and cardboard boxes dumped against one wall. God! He really didn't want to hide amongst that lot, but the squeaking and rattling of the shopping trolley grew louder and louder. Reluctantly Jacob crouched down and squeezed between the bags.

If only he hadn't shouted at her all those years ago, he wouldn't be in this mess. But you might as well say if only his parents hadn't separated, he wouldn't have stormed out of the house and been moping around the fountain when she turned up with that bloody trolley. But they had, and he had, and she had. And now, every time she saw him, she ran away screaming, just like she had done that day.

The smell of damp cardboard, the acrid plastic of the refuse sacks, and the deeply unpleasant scent of whatever was inside filled Jacob's nostrils. Bollocks, this wasn't how he would have chosen to spend the night, but it was better than an encounter with the Queen.

Out in the street, the rattling of her trolley grew louder before squeaking to a halt. Jacob strained to hear what was happening outside the doorway. Footsteps approached. Screwing up his nose, he slid a slimy sheet of cardboard over his head and burrowed deeper beneath the rubbish bags. For fuck's sake! This was all his bloody dad's fault - all that bollocks about another world, that was the real reason his parents had split up. Why couldn't he have kept his mouth shut and just been normal like everyone else?

The footsteps stopped. Jacob risked a glance out. Shit! She was standing right there, in the entrance to the alley. Shit, shit, shit! She couldn't have seen him, there was no way she'd get this close if she had. What if she was looking for somewhere to sleep? He could be stuck here all night.

The scraping of her shoes across the paving stones was loud in the night; she was getting closer. Her fragile, bird-like twittering filtered through the rubbish bags. "Not here dear, no, no, we won't find it here." What was that? Movement, right above him. No! She was moving things around, rummaging through the boxes.

Something dropped down on top of the pile. "Oh dear me no, this will never do. This will not get us back." The words were quieter, further away. Thank Christ for that. She must have moved to the other side of the alley. Perhaps she was going back to her trolley.

Jacob's heart was thumping, and his foot was going numb too. If he didn't move it soon it'd hurt like hell when the feeling came back. He eased it to one side, slowly... slowly... just the tiniest amount... The mound of bags shifted and dropped. Shit! Outside, everything went quiet. Then more shuffling, closer and closer. The rubbish sacks covering him moved again. She was burrowing in! He closed his eyes and held his breath. Please don't let her see me. It's dark. Maybe she won't see me.

"Ooh!" she said. "And what do have we here?"

This was it. She'd found him. Jacob tensed, waiting for the piercing scream that would accompany his discovery.

A second passed...

Another...

He opened his eyes a fraction, squinting out into the alleyway. It was deserted. The Queen had moved away and was now standing at the fountain, touching the stonework all over with her fingertips, cooing and clucking. She pulled a rolled-up paper bag from a ledge, carefully unwrapped it, and started tucking cold chips into her mouth. Oh, for Christ's sake. The chips! She'd come for the bloody chips. She'd never know it was him who left them for her, but it made Jacob feel better - but he wasn't supposed to still be here when she came for them.

A few minutes later, the Queen of England rolled up her paper bag, placed it very precisely back on the ledge, and left in the direction of the train station. He was safe.

Jacob emerged from the alley, brushing debris from his clothes. He was a state, but the Queen had it far worse. She might be a royal pain in the arse, but she deserved better; a woman of her age alone on the streets. He'd only been out for a couple of hours and he was bloody freezing.

The rattling of the Queen's trolley had faded away. It had been close, but if he was going to make it into work tomorrow, he'd better get back home to bed.

CHAPTER 4

Many things were a mystery to The-man-who-didn't-know-who-he-was. He didn't know, for example, if he had always lived in the beautiful, but deserted city strung between the tree trunks high in the forest, but he hoped he had.

Another thing the man didn't know was why the city was deserted. It didn't seem very likely that it had been built solely for him, and yet the houses and the walkways and the gathering places and the libraries were all unoccupied. For as long as he could remember— which didn't seem to be very long, but it was hard to be sure— he'd been able to wander the city at his leisure and in all that time had never once encountered another living soul.

Each morning as the mist rose from the forest floor, the man set out hoping this would be the day when he found someone who could tell him who he was and why he had no memory. And each evening as constellations of fireflies gathered between the trees, he returned to the house that might always have been his feeling like he was the only man in the world.

And then, one day, when the man returned from his explorations, he stepped from the walkway outside his house and stopped. He tapped his fingers rhythmically against his chin and chewed on his bottom lip. Amongst all the things the man didn't know, there was one thing of which he was certain, and that was when he left this morning, he'd closed the door.

He peered into the darkness and listened, and when he heard nothing he slipped cautiously inside. Something was different. Subtle currents moved through the air; he wouldn't even have noticed if the house hadn't always been so still. The room was filled with the kind of silence that only happens when something is trying not to make a sound, and something in the quality of the shadows suggested they concealed more than just a table and chairs.

"I was wondering when you would return," said a voice.

CHAPTER 5

Liam scowled at the sky and pulled his coat tighter around him as he made his way down Pike Street hill. Overhead, dark, heavy clouds gathered, and distant thunder grumbled and complained like a dreaming dog. It wasn't raining yet, but it would be, and soon.

All around him people glanced nervously upwards and hurried into the shops for shelter. The sharp smell of impending rain permeated the air, but still there was no sign of Daisy anywhere on the hill. He could just imagine the reaction if he'd been late instead of her. He glanced up again and tutted. There was no way she'd arrive before the first drops began to fall.

The previous evening, Daisy had sent him a series of text messages asking to meet up this morning. She wouldn't say why, but Liam was left in no doubt that none of his excuses would be good enough get him out of it. Even his attempt to renegotiate the time to so he could at least have a lie-in had been refused, and still she wasn't here.

Although Liam had only been in his new job for a matter of weeks, he and Daisy found they enjoyed each other's company straight away. Their shared healthy disrespect for work was one of the few things that made going in more than just a chore. Even so, she had gone to some lengths to ensure Liam understood that he was not her type. Liam had assured her with a smile that she didn't need to concern herself, because she simply wasn't that hot. They had been firm friends ever since.

About mid-way down the hill, Liam heard Daisy calling him. It didn't sound like this was her first attempt to get his attention. In addition to her other qualities, Daisy was not the most patient of people, it wouldn't do to keep her waiting, even if she was the one who was late.

"Alright Daise?" said Liam, "Sorry, I was miles away. How's things?"

"Yeah, not bad thanks," she replied. "Look, shall we go to Java Joe's? We're going to get soaked any minute, we can get a coffee and something to eat, I'm starved."

Liam and Daisy set off towards the café just as the first isolated drops of rain began to fall. Apart from someone sheltering in a doorway further down the hill, the street was now empty. Liam glanced over as they drew close. The guy in the doorway didn't look too good, leaning heavily against the window, with his chest heaving like he couldn't catch his breath. And there was something else too, had they been at school together? No, Liam would have remembered, but there was something…

"Come on!" urged Daisy, tugging on Liam's arm. "Do you actually want to get wet?"

Liam glanced back as Daisy led him away. Perhaps it was the storm, but he was starting to feel a bit rough himself. It was so bloody hot, and he felt like he was going to throw up. He pulled down the zip of his jacket and fanned his face with his hands; it didn't help. Hopefully it was just the humidity, and everything would be fine once the storm broke.

"Liam, what the hell's wrong with you?" Daisy tugged on his arm, causing him to blink and look up at her.

"What?"

"Really? You've stopped moving, we'll get drenched!"

"Sorry Daisy. Look, I don't feel too good, I..."

God, he really didn't. Thunder crashed overhead, and Liam screwed his eyes closed, pressing his knuckles hard against his temples. His head was splitting - the rain couldn't come quick enough.

Daisy placed a hand on each side of Liam's face and turned him towards her, examining him closely. "Are you okay? 'Cos you look like crap. Come on, you'll feel better once you've eaten."

"What? Oh, sorry. Yeah. Java Joe's. Great idea." It was getting hard to even think straight, and his legs felt like they were made of lead. He needed to sit down before they gave way on him. Daisy was right. Get to the café. Something to eat and a shot of coffee. That'd help.

Thrusting her arm through his, Daisy steered him down the hill, pulling him close to the buildings and out of the worst of the rain. "Don't read too much into this you," she said with a smile, "I twisted my ankle a bit on my way up the hill that's all, you're just a convenient support."

Liam tried to force a chuckle in response. It was no good, he felt terrible, he needed to sit down. "Daise, look, I…"

At that moment, the lurid pink handbag slung over Daisy's arm began to emit a rhythmic buzzing. She stopped, and pulled her arm free of Liam's, guiding him down until he was sitting on the curb. After a short rattling search, she fished her phone out of her bag.

Daisy's voice echoed around the thumping in his head. "It's you," she said, "you're butt-dialing me."

Liam slumped forward and leaned his head against his knees. Immediately, his headache began to ease, and the nauseating heat dissipated. Bloody hell, was that all he needed to do? Just sit down for a moment and he'd feel better? Daisy had been talking - something about him calling her. He pulled his phone from his pocket and waved it vaguely in her direction "No, I'm not. It's off, look."

"Oh, feeling better then?" That was more like the usual Daisy. Her earlier concern had been a little out of character, but he really did feel better.

Daisy squatted next to him and turned her phone to face him. Across the middle of the screen the words: "Liam (work)" were rapidly being obscured by drops of rain.

Liam showed her the blank screen of his own phone. "See?"

"Well, that's weird," said Daisy. "I suppose I'd better answer it." As soon as she said it, the screen went dark.

"It's rung off," she said. "Must've been a glitch. Come on, let's get you something to eat before my mascara starts to run."

"Your mascara? Good to see you've got your priorities straight. I'm sitting in a bloody puddle here. The arse of my jeans is soaked through."

At the bottom of the hill Liam stopped. "Hang on a sec, I just want to check something." He turned and walked back to the shop entrance. That guy in the doorway... Liam couldn't put his finger on it, but... well, hopefully he was feeling better now too. He'd hate for something to happen to him, but he must have recovered too because the doorway was empty.

Daisy placed two lattes down on the table, slid one over to Liam, and dragged out a chair.

"Jacob?" said Liam, "Really?"

"And?" said Daisy.

"*Jacob* - Jacob? JJ?"

"Of course *Jacob* - Jacob. Who the hell did you think I meant?"

"But… Jacob."

"Shut up," said Daisy, "I'm not asking you to go out with him."

"No, but you dragged me out of bed for this. Couldn't you have just called?"

"S'pose, but at least you get a coffee out of it this way, anyway, it'll do you good to get out of bed before lunchtime. Well…?"

"Well what?"

"Oh, for God's sake Liam, are you going to make me spell it out? Do you think he… you know… likes me?"

CHAPTER 6

"What ya doin' retard?"

What? Who the hell said that? Jacob squinted in the unexpected, yellow glare. He was under Fountain, but... but that couldn't be right – he'd fallen asleep in front of the T.V. How could he be... He rubbed his eyes, and a bulky, thick-necked figure swam into focus, blocking his path. "Davy?" Jacob croaked. His mouth was dry, and his lips felt like they belonged to someone else; thick, sluggish, and unresponsive. "What the... what are you doing here?"

Martin Davy leered at him. Jacob glanced right. Andrew Beckerleg - there was no mistaking that pinched face and scruffy brown hair. Two girls were clinging on to his arms, wobbling on high-heels and spilling out of their too-tight tops. Shit, he'd been sleepwalking again. How the hell was he going to get out of it this time?

"I asked you a question." Davy emphasised his final word by raising both hands and pushing Jacob hard in the chest. Jacob staggered backwards and slammed into the fountain. Pain burned across his back.

Beckerleg's eyes were glassy and vague, and he was wavering about slightly as if he couldn't quite retain his balance. A half-drunk bottle of beer dangled from his fingers. He wouldn't be too much of a problem. But Davy… Davy looked intent on causing trouble.

"Still can't handle your drink then?" said Jacob. It probably wasn't going to help; about the only thing that Davy was good at was holding his alcohol.

"Shut up Trevorrow, I may have been drinking, but at least I'm not the one sleeping in the street. You and your family are making the whole town look like bloody idiots. Like father, like son, I'd say."

Every bloody time! Whenever Jacob was in any trouble, his dad was always in there somewhere, and Davy would always bring it up. Maybe it was time to shake things up a bit. Jacob looked over to the two women. "Come on girls, show a bit of class. You can do better than these two losers." Also not going to help, but it already looked unlikely that this would end well.

"Swear to God Trevorrow, if you don't shut that mouth of yours…"

Glass shattered as the bottle fell from Beckerleg's fingers and exploded against the granite flagstones. He staggered sideways, gazing stupidly down at his hand. Davy spun round. "Fuck's sake Andrew, an' you're a bloody embarrassment too." Beckerleg didn't appear to notice.

Davy's neck was starting to go red – that was never a good sign. He'd had already proved he was prepared to cross the boundary between verbal insults and physical contact. He wasn't going to let this go. But perhaps there was a way… Everyone knew Jacob wasn't a fighter. The last thing Davy would expect was for Jacob to hit him. After all, it'd never happened before, but the shove and the unexpected smack in the back from the fountain had set his adrenaline flowing.

Davy might not be as wasted as Beckerleg, but he was still drunk, how good could his reactions be?

Jacob was fooling himself; he wasn't going to hit anyone. What if he did some serious damage? And if he didn't, even if he just knocked him down, Davy still wouldn't let it go. He'd turn it into a vendetta. His reputation was all he had - he couldn't afford to lose that.

There was another way though.

A sinister smile spread slowly across Jacob's face. He snorted and shook his head. "You really are a fuck-wit Davy. Fine, have it your way. Wanna say your good-byes to the girls now? You know, while you still have a bit of self-respect left?"

CHAPTER 7

Flashes of sunlight sparkled from the river, and Liam squinted against the glare. It was a lovely spot - strange he'd never been here before. Perhaps he'd wandered off course a bit.; he had been walking for a while. But... what if he was lost? A cold tingling crawled over his back; you wouldn't want to be lost in a place like this. If he could just retrace his steps, he could get back to the town... Wait, where was it? He chewed on his fingers and scanned around. There it was, in the shadow of those dark mountains. Christ, they were huge; had they always been there? Wouldn't he have remembered if Liskeard was ringed by mountains like that? Maybe he should take a closer look before heading home.

The sheer black flank of the mountain loomed over him. Liam blinked and took a step backwards. What the...? How the hell did that happen? He was at the base of the mountain, but he'd been miles away, and then, the moment he thought about it, he was right beneath it. Reaching out, he slid his hand over the black, glassy surface, a subtle ridging rippled beneath his fingers - obsidian. He looked back over his shoulder. The town was gone.

This place - the way it kept changing, the way time and distance meant nothing - it was... shit, what was it? It was completely freaky and alien, and yet... some hidden part of him knew how it worked. What the hell was it? It wasn't... it wasn't a... a dream, was it?

Suddenly, words poured into his mind, they smelled of rain and tasted of metal. Brilliant, iridescent blue flashed before his eyes. Liam spun around. It was coming from everywhere at once. "What? Who's there? What did you say?"

"We need you. Your friend needs you."

"What? Who... who are you? Why do you need me?"

"Oh, come now Liam, you know who I am, do you not?"

Well, yeah, he kind of did, from when he'd been here before. K... something, wasn't it? Kasandra - something like that? "Look, I'm not sure I can help you Ker... Keren... I mean, how can I help? I don't even know if I'm asleep or not."

"It's Kerenza," said the voice-colour-smell, "and you most certainly are asleep Liam, it is the only way I can talk to you at present."

Kerenza, yeah, that sounded right. He did know that name. "Really? I'm asleep? Does that mean I'm having a lucid dream?"

"It is certainly possible. Only you would know that though, it is your dream after all." Liam looked around again. Was he dreaming? Damn, it was so hard to tell. Kerenza spoke again. "You cannot stay here Liam. We need you. Your friend needs you. You have to wake up."

The voice was very insistent, and Liam's heart began to race.

"Liam! You have to wake up right now!"

God, he wanted to. He really wanted to wake up. But by now he was high on the mountain. How the hell did he get up here? It was sickeningly, dizzyingly real and there was no way down. Every handhold, every foothold was just out of reach. He screwed his eyes closed and pressed himself close in against the rockface.

"Liam! Wake up!"

Wind howled around him in a black sky filled with rain and stinging ice. Liam's foot slipped on the wet stone, and his stomach lurched. He fell, grabbing at a broken piece of obsidian. The wavering edge cut easily into the soft flesh of his palm, the spurt of blood making the rock slippery. The handhold slipped through his fingers, slicing through skin and tendons, until it scraped across hard bone. He tried to scream, but it was a feeble rattle in his throat.

A drop of blood rolled out between his ruined fingers and fell away towards the distant ground.

The scream took form.

His limbs reacted.

Tangled up in his duvet, Liam flew backwards along his bed and banged his head into the wall behind him.

His ragged breathing slowed to a rhythmic pant as the flash of adrenaline faded. His hand! Christ, it had been sliced wide open! Wincing, he risked a glance through eyes squeezed almost shut. It was fine. There was nothing there but an old scar on his palm, right where the rock had cut through in the dream. Funny how he couldn't remember where it had come from. Reaching out to his bedside table he picked up his phone. The display flickered into life causing him to squint.

Three thirty.

Faint echoes reverberated around the room. Were they just in his mind? "We need you. Your friend needs you..."

Liam rolled over and closed his eyes, but it was already too late, and he knew it. His mind was filling with questions, each one dragging him further from sleep.

And who the hell was… what was her name again? Cadence? Kredensa? When he'd been dreaming, he really felt like he knew her in the same way that he felt like he knew the place he'd dreamed of. Now that he was awake, he wasn't so sure.

With a sigh he threw off the duvet, swung his legs over the side of the bed and wandered over to the window.

The familiar view along the road was made dangerous and strange by the yellow streetlights and absence of people. But there was someone, there, at the bottom of the hill. It was unusual enough to see anyone out in the streets at this time of night, but the way this person moved, the way they were dressed. Memories of things that had never happened were stirred up from the settling silt of his dreams. It was the woman he had been dreaming of! Kerenza, of course, that was her name. For a moment he just stared.

Shit! You might not know when you're dreaming, but you damned sure know when you're awake. Liam Verren was definitely awake, and the woman he had been dreaming of was still there, outside in the road, waiting.

What the hell was happening? Grabbing his t-shirt from the floor, Liam tripped out of his room struggling to pull his jeans up. With his heartbeat pounding in his ears he flew down the communal stairway and out of the front door.

In the middle of the road he thumped to a halt. Kerenza was gone.

He was not, however, alone. From the top of the hill drifted the sound of raised voices.

CHAPTER 8

"Don't be a twat Davy."

Martin Davy spun round. For fuck's sake! Liam Verren as well? What the hell was he doing here? It had to be after three in the morning. "Piss off Verren, this is nothing to do with you."

"Come on man." Liam edged closer to where Martin had Jacob pinned against the fountain. "Don't do this, you're better than that, leave him alone."

It was smart arsed comments like that were going to get Verren a smack in the mouth. Always thought he was so bloody clever. He wouldn't look too clever with a black eye now, would he? Yeah, he could easily take both of them, no problem, even without Beckerleg. That idiot never could handle his drink.

Jacob took a step away from the fountain. "Liam, look, I appreciate the help and everything, but it's okay. I've got this."

"You sure JJ? Because it really doesn't look like it."

"Yeah, I'm sure. Look it's not often this moron says anything worth listening to, but on this occasion, I'd do what he says. You don't want to get hurt."

Martin took a swig of beer from his bottle. What the actual…? They'd always been mouthy. Trevorrow never knew when to shut the hell up. but the pair of them were chatting away like he wasn't even here. Fuck it, Verren was going to get his. He stepped towards him.

Jacob snapped his fingers. "Hey, Davy! Over here. What's the matter? You had too much to drink or something?"

Martin shook his head and took a long look at the bottle. That little wanker might be right. Still, too much to drink or not, he'd had enough of their shit. He clenched his fist and turned back towards Liam. Jacob moved with him. What was he playing at now? He was dancing around like a moron. Every time Martin moved Jacob was with him smiling and staring him straight in the eye. Shit, now he'd forgotten what he was doing. He'd been going to do something, hadn't he? What hell was it? Something to do with Amy and Tigan? Yeah, that could've been it - the girls. Might be better to just go off with them.

"I think you're right Martin, it is a good idea," Martin blinked. Jacob was right in front of him, his eyes were inches from Martin's own. And the way he was smiling – that was just plain weird.

"Huh?" said Martin stepping back. "Right 'bout what? What's a good idea?"

"Going with the girls. Screw us, we're losers, not worth it. It'd be a shame to ruin a good evening."

Yeah, it was a bloody good idea. An' at least it'd put a bit of distance between him and that freak Trevorrow. Jesus, what's in this bloody beer? Must be a bad pint or something… Still, people didn't usually give him credit for much. 'Specially not Trevorrow. He wasn't going to say he'd had an idea as good as that if he hadn't.

Off to his left, a retching followed by an unpleasant splattering sound rang clearly through the night air as Beckerleg voided his stomach contents over the pavement.

The two girls shrieked and jumped backwards away from the doubled over and still heaving form of Beckerleg.

Shit, that was all he needed. The girls weren't going to hang around after that. "Bloody hell, Andrew, what the fuck's the matter with you? You trying to ruin our chances?"

"Oh God," said Tigan. "He's thrown up on my shoes! Come on Amy let's go."

Martin frowned and looked from Jacob to Liam. Where the hell had these two turned up from again? Wait a minute! He could hear chattering, fading into the night. He spun round scowling. Shit. The girls! In the distance two figures were tottering away. "Amy, Tigan, Wait up! It's just him, he's a fricking idiot, he can find his own way home."

Martin broke into a loping jog and puffed up the street after them.

"So, you wanna tell me what the hell that was all about?" said Liam as he and Jacob started to walk down Pike Street hill towards their homes.

"That? Oh, nothing really. You know Davy, he's always been an idiot. It doesn't take much to set him off."

"I meant the way you dealt with it. Telling me to not get involved and then, I don't know, the way you talked him out of it, it was weird."

"What? He was pissed. He didn't know what he was doing. Probably just forgot he was being an arse."

Jacob was being evasive. Something didn't quite add up, but Liam was too tired to argue about it. And anyway, he'd got his own issues to deal with. Issues concerning dreams that carried on after he had woken up. "I've got to ask," said

Liam, "what were you doing out here in the middle of the night anyway?"

"Couldn't sleep. I got so fed up just lying there in bed that I decided to get out for a bit of a walk."

That didn't seem right either. Jacob was no stranger to late nights, thanks to his love of computer games, but walking and fresh air? That was new. And anyway, he didn't look like someone who couldn't sleep, he looked a lot more like someone could— dazed expression, messed up hair, crumpled clothes— and where was his beanie hat? He was almost never seen without that.

"I could ask you the same thing." Jacob continued.

That was a subject Liam didn't want to consider in any more detail right now. In the dream he'd known Jacob was in some kind of trouble. Had he known though, or did someone tell him? He couldn't quite remember. Actually, he couldn't remember too much about it at all now. And since all that trouble with Jacob's dad going off the rails, even the hint of anything remotely weird was likely to seriously piss Jacob off. He'd be better off not mentioning the dream at all. It was probably nothing to worry about. At least he hoped it wasn't.

"Just been waking up in the middle of the night lately," said Liam. "Don't know why. I heard shouting and went to the window. I thought it looked like you, so I came out to investigate.

"Anyway," said Liam as they arrived at the bottom of the hill, "this is me,"

"Twat!" Jacob laughed and pushed Liam away. "See you tomorrow?"

"Yeah," said Liam, "Maybe."

CHAPTER 9

In the few days since Liam intervened in the altercation between Davy, Beckerleg, and Jacob, Kerenza confined herself to his dreams. Her brief appearance in the street outside his flat had been bothering him rather more than he liked to admit; the cast of your dreams don't generally trouble the real world, not unless there's something pretty wrong with you mentally. But, with the benefit of a little distance, he'd been able to calm down and think things through. He wasn't so sure he really had been awake. Awake enough to get out of bed and run down the stairs, granted, but not fully conscious. And there'd been that article he'd read online somewhere, about a stage of sleep where people felt that they were still awake. That must've been what happened.

It was better than confronting the other distressing possibilities.

Liam gazed out of the bus window, lulled by the rumbling and whining of the engine. An evening at the pub the night before had ended up with him staying overnight at Daisy's place after he missed the last bus back. He could have just called Jacob and asked for a lift, but it seemed a bit cheeky since they hadn't asked him along. And so, Liam sat and watched the stunted gorse bushes, granite boulders, and scruffy, wind-blasted sheep pass by as the bus bounced and jolted its way back towards town.

The journey took an age, stopping in every village, where almost no one got on and almost no one got off. He really should have asked for that lift. Pushing his earbuds into his ears, Liam closed his eyes.

Allowing himself to drift off and become absorbed in his playlist proved so effective that he barely noticed when the bus rattled over the cattle grid as it left the moorland. And later was mildly surprised to see the town centre passing outside the window when the music ended. He stuffed his earbuds into his jacket pocket, content to gaze out for the final few minutes of the journey.

There were so many people in the town that day that Liam couldn't take them all in. The scene outside dissolved into a blur of cars, shopfronts, shopping-bags and designer tee-shirts - a pair of green eyes, the turn of a head, the flow of a cape.

Liam spun around in his seat, his face pressed close to the glass, straining to see as the bus pulled further away. No! His pulse banged in his head, and all the fears he'd been battling came flooding back.

It was her!

She stared straight at him. Then, the instant she was sure he'd seen her, or so it seemed, she broke eye contact, turned and moved away. As she headed in the direction of Pike Street hill, the other shoppers stepped aside, allowing her to pass. That wouldn't happen if she was a dream.

Liam jumped up out of his seat and ran for the door. The driver was already slowing down, and the other passengers were beginning to stir in their seats. But Kerenza was walking away before the bus had even begun to slow. Liam couldn't afford to get stuck behind anyone: that elderly couple who would struggle to get off the bus and then stop and thank the driver, or that woman with the pushchair negotiating with her toddler to get back in. Liam felt a stab of guilt as he dodged and sidestepped quickly down the aisle of the bus. On any other day he would have waited for them to get off first.

The bus shuddered to a stop, the brakes hissing like they'd been holding their breath for the whole journey. Just inside the door a woman bent over, clucking and fussing as she tried to untangle herself from the lead of her excited handbag dog. Come on! Liam dodged from side to side, looking for a way past before vaulting right over them. Moments later he was racing back along the road to where he'd last seen Kerenza at the top of the hill.

She was gone. He spun around on the spot, the faces of the shoppers whirling past as he searched for her. Then he had her - halfway down the hill - still walking away.

He trotted after her; he didn't want to frighten her away. Frighten her? What a joke! He was the one who should be scared. There were only a couple of good reasons for seeing someone he'd previously only dreamed of in the real world. Neither of those options stirred any emotion other than fear: either he was going crazy, or someone had drugged him. He wasn't sure which was worse.

Half-elated at the prospect of catching up with her and half-terrified he was losing his mind; Liam began to close the gap.

The world warped.

Liam stumbled to a halt. What the… The familiar architecture of Liskeard rippled and flowed, like the town was projected onto a curtain. White stone, glass, and flowering trees flickered into being. The dressed granite of the museum, Guild Hall, and shop fronts were gone. And then just as quickly it was all back. Liam twisted around, but each time he caught a ripple, the vision swung away from him. It was like a dream. The harder he looked, the harder it was to see. With each new transformation the sounds of everyday life faded away, replaced by the gurgling of water. Not only that, but the sounds were colours and the colours had scent and texture.

Jesus H Christ! What the hell was going on? A minute ago, he was bored half out of his mind on the bus and now suddenly he was having some kind of breakdown. The only constant was Kerenza. Liam stumbled after her, trying to ignore the dewy grass brushing over his shoes where there should have been pavement. Then even she wasn't there anymore. Wait, yes, she was, but only if he didn't look directly at her. She solidified again at the bottom of the hill, turning onto Fore Street. Liam staggered around the corner after her. Without changing her stride, Kerenza was now at least thirty yards ahead of him.

Liskeard snapped back. Liam broke into a sprint; he had to catch up now, while he could still see. Shoppers turned and stared after him, their offended huffs swirling in his wake. Drawing level with the short alley down to the well, Kerenza stopped and turned to face him.

Thoughts crowded into his mind, jostling for attention. This was madness. What if it was the start of some permanent change? He could be trapped in this bizarre half-world forever. And what must people be thinking as he stumbled past, eyes wide and panting, pursuing someone who in all probability wasn't even there?

Kerenza held out her hand.

Liam ran harder.

A half smile flickered across Kerenza's lips as the green of her eyes, the copper of her hair and the deep burgundy of her cloak dissolved and flowed out into the air.

Liam stopped. He was standing in the Fore Street that he'd always known. The bizarre rippling in the air was gone.

And so was Kerenza.

CHAPTER 10

Liam groaned and dropped his phone back down on the bedside table. The call suggesting a visit to Java Joe's was not exactly out of character for Jacob. His taste for strong, black coffee— freshly ground and Italian— was well known. The timing was a different matter. Would the café even be open at eight thirty on a Saturday morning? Jacob wasn't one for getting up early on his days off. There was another thing too; Java Joe's was at the bottom of Pike Street. Liam hadn't been that way since the day he'd chased after Kerenza, and he'd been trying not think about that. Jacob had sounded worried though, there might be more to it than simple caffeine stabilisation— he'd probably better go and find out what was up.

Perhaps Jacob wanted to meet because he also had a secret crush on Daisy. That would simplify things a bit; the two of them could get up as early as they liked, go out for coffee and leave Liam to enjoy his sleep. Unfortunately, it probably wasn't going to be that easy. No, this was far more likely to be related to the night-time incident with Davy and

Beckerleg at the fountain last weekend. What the hell had that been about anyway?

Liam grunted and rolled off the bed; there was only one way to find out.

Pike Street. This was where it had happened. Liam trailed his fingers along the wall. It felt solid enough. The few other people on the hill seemed to be sticking to the rules; no one was disappearing or dissolving into the air.

A short way beyond the turning into Fore Street, a figure rounded the corner. The beanie hat pulled tightly down over the lank black hair and the slow rolling walk were instantly familiar— Jacob. It was good to see him again. Until that moment, Liam hadn't realised just how much. So far, he'd told precisely no one about the bizarre events that had been freaking him out.

"Jacob!" There was no response. Liam raised his voice. "Jacob! JJ!"

On the other side of the road Jacob looked up, pulled an earbud from one ear, and waved. "Alright Liam?"

"S'pose. You?"

Jacob ambled across the road. His face was pale beneath his black fringe and the skin under each eye was as dark as a faded bruise. It looked like Liam wasn't the only one with things on his mind. They gripped each other's hands and bumped shoulders.

"Bloody hell mate," said Liam. "You look like crap."

"Yeah, thanks buddy," said Jacob, sarcastically. "You're looking good too."

Liam smiled and placed an arm around his friend's shoulders. "Hey, if you can't trust me to tell it to you like it is, then who can you trust?"

Jacob smiled back, but it wasn't his usual easy grin, the one that seemed to flow straight from his soul. This one looked forced and weak. His mouth said he was fine, but his face told a different story. Liam was right. This was about more than just coffee. "Come on, we'd better get you to the café, you look like a man with unnaturally high levels of blood in your caffeine system."

At a cramped two-person table by the window, Liam idly swiped at the screen of his mobile phone, while Jacob gazed into the curls of steam drifting up from his coffee. If he was hoping to read the future from it, it either wasn't working, or he didn't like what he saw there. It might be best not to mention his own worries just now. Jacob seemed to have enough on his mind without Liam adding to it.

"Okay," said Liam. "Let's have it then. What's up? You've got me out of bed and down here at this ungodly hour of the morning. You may as well just tell me what it is."

Jacob slurped a mouthful of coffee. "I dunno really, I suppose I just er… I kind of…"

"Come on mate, spit it out. Is this something to do with Daisy?"

Jacob stopped with his mug halfway to his mouth. "What? Your mate Daisy? No. Where the hell did you get that from? Why would I be worried about Daisy?"

Oops. Okay then, so apparently not Daisy. She wouldn't be happy when she found out he'd let the cat out of the bag. "No reason. Look, forget I said anything, okay?"

"Well, I can't do that now, can I? What do you mean *is it something to do with Daisy*? Has she said something?"

"Yes. I mean no. Well, kind of. Look can we just get back to why we're here?"

"Yeah. Okay, then," said Jacob, "right after the bit where you tell me what Daisy said."

"Christ, JJ. I'm not supposed to say anything. You can't let her know I told you, okay? You don't know her like I do. She'll tear me a new one if she finds out."

"And?"

"Well, look, let's just say if you asked her out, she might not say no."

"Fuck," said Jacob shaking his head slowly.

"Probably a bit too early to say," said Liam, "but, long term, who knows?"

Jacob laughed and cuffed Liam with his beanie hat. "It wasn't a question you twat."

"Okay," said Liam, "your turn. What did you want to talk about?"

"Shit, I don't know man, it's probably nothing…" Jacob glanced quickly from side to side then leaned in close to Liam across the table. "Look, do you ever, you know, go to sleep in one place and then, when you wake up…"

On the other side of café, cutlery clattered down on to a plate, and a chair scraped noisily across the floor. Jacob twitched and turned to watch the customer leave.

"Come on JJ, I got up early for this."

"Oh, look, it's nothing really mate. I can't sleep, that's all. Pretty much every night it seems. I wake up about three in the morning, and either don't get back off, or fall asleep five minutes before the alarm."

"And that's it? That's what's bothering you?"

"Well, you said I looked like crap. Now you know why."

There was clearly more to this than just not sleeping. It sounded like Jacob had been sleepwalking, and it fitted in with that business with Davy at the fountain. But, if he refused to talk about it, what could Liam do? He deliberately hadn't told Jacob about his own issues, which, given that there was a very real possibility he could be losing his mind, were considerably more worrying than a bit of insomnia. Maybe he should tell him anyway, one of them should show a bit of trust. Then again, perhaps JJ just needed a bit of time. If he was so worried that he felt he couldn't talk about it, well wasn't that just the same way Liam was feeling? Yeah, he'd leave it for now, give JJ the benefit of the doubt. There'd be other times.

Liam took a large mouthful of his coffee. "Damn!" he said as the hot liquid scalded his mouth. He swallowed it quickly, almost dropping the mug back down onto the table. Jacob raised his eyes from his own mug in concern.

"Alright?"

"Yeah, too hot is all. I'll live. Look, this not sleeping business, I doubt it's anything serious, you know, like anything physically wrong, more likely to be something psychological."

Jacob slurped another a mouthful of hot coffee, rattling it past his teeth. "It could be that." Liam nodded at Jacob's cup. "You do get through a hell of a lot of coffee. Maybe if you laid off it for a while you might sleep better."

"Yeah, you could be right, I'll give it some consideration." Jacob drained the last of his coffee. He didn't look like a man planning on cutting back any time soon. "Look, seriously, thanks for meeting up mate, I do feel a bit better now, you know, for talking it through."

Liam looked at Jacob over his mug. Yeah, right. Just a bout of insomnia? No bloody way.

CHAPTER 11

An insistent vibration pulsed against Liam's leg. He pulled his phone from his pocket. It was Daisy. Bloody hell, that was quick, he'd only left Java Joe's after his coffee with Jacob a matter of seconds ago.

"You stalking me or something?" he said.
"What? No! What're you talking about Liam?"
"Sorry, bad joke. What's up?"
"Did you talk to him? Jacob?"
"Kind of."
"What do you mean *Kind of*?"
"Look, I know you want me to find out if he likes you, but... well, it's complicated, he's got a load of other stuff going on right now. It wasn't really the right time." Not strictly true, but also technically not a lie.
"Stuff? Stuff like what?"
"I'm not sure. I just got the feeling he was keeping something back."

"Really? Do you think he's okay?" There was a worried edge to her voice. Daisy was usually so self-assured and confident; she must have it bad.

"Well, he seemed better when I left, so yeah, I think so." He didn't really think so, but Liam had problems of his own to deal with, and he could do without Daisy badgering him as well.

There was too much to think about— whatever it was that was bothering Jacob, Jacob and Daisy, not to mention the whole am-I-going-to-be-spending-the-rest-of-my-life-under-specialist-medical-care thing. Christ, that'd be bad enough on its own, and now it seemed he was having to tread carefully around Daisy too.

He'd intended to go straight home from the café, then Daisy had called, and now, absorbed in his thoughts, he was wandering around aimlessly.

"Liam!" Daisy's voice rang in his left ear. "Are you actually listening to a word I am saying?"

Crap, she was still speaking. "Yeah, yeah, 'course I am," he replied, rapidly replaying the last few seconds of their conversation in his mind. "I'm in town, though, crossing the road, there's a lot of traffic." If Daisy had the slightest suspicion that he hadn't followed every detail of what she was saying, she'd feel compelled to start again. In fact, even if she did believe he was paying attention, there was no guarantee she wouldn't restate everything again anyway, just to be sure that he fully understood. Better to be cautious, even if it did involve a little white lie.

"Look Daise, I'm really not comfortable talking about this stuff. You do know I'm a guy, right? We like to suppress our feelings, and we never, ever talk about them. Ever."

Liam drifted left to avoid a small knot of shoppers. The narrow alleyway he found himself in inclined gently downward beneath his feet, and the background noise of the town began to diminish.

He was almost at the bottom of the alley that ran between the Fore Street shopping arcade and Well Lane, close to the old pipe well. No wonder it was so quiet. He'd wandered a bit further from home than he'd thought, but, no biggie, a left turn at the end of the alley past the well would bring him to the bottom of Pike Street. He could head back from there.

"Look Daise, I think you're just gonna have to speak to him yourself, and I don't mean over the phone. You'll never get through to him if he's near a computer. I'm not going to be much help to you to be honest, guys are really bad at…"

A chill crawled across his back. Liam stiffened, as a soft breath blew across the back of his neck. Someone was right behind him.

He froze. A distant voice still sounded from his phone. "Liam? Liam? Are you still there?"

Slowly he began to turn around, his hair prickling. Shit, oh shit! There was someone there.

The road was empty.

But there had been someone. He knew it as well as if they had been looking him in the eye.

The Pipe Well.

There was nowhere else they could have gone.

Liam looked up and down the lane. Where the hell was everyone?

He edged closer to the well, his footsteps muffled and distant, drowned out by the thumping in his ears. He squeezed his fingernails deep into his palms. It didn't stop his hands from shaking. Slowly, he crossed the last few feet to the stairs leading to the underground chamber that housed the well.

There was someone down there.

In the semi-darkness at the opposite end of the chamber, gazing down into the water, stood a woman. The hood of her cloak was pushed back high on her head, and cascades of auburn hair framed her face. Liam blinked back a jolt of recognition.

Kerenza.

He sucked in a ragged breath and clamped his hand over his mouth; even that small sound might break the spell keeping her here. Steadying himself against the wall, he began to descend the stairs on trembling legs.

Kerenza continued to stare into the trough of water, as Liam stepped off the final stair on onto the floor of the chamber. Why didn't she look up? She must know he was here. A hint of a smile turned up the sides of her mouth. Liam paused, something about the way she smiled was…

"Hello Liam."

An explosion of colour blazed and flared around her words, and the room filled with the scent of lilies. Jesus Christ! Liam staggered backwards, stumbling into the wall of the chamber. His senses overwhelmed, he scrambled backwards, but there was just the wall. Where were the stairs? He had to get out! Lurching to the side, he tripped and fell to his knees, blinded and drowning in the fragrance of flowers.

The aroma and colours drained away, seeping through the gaps between the stones. The chamber reappeared around him. The rough slate walls, the trough of water, the stairs. The stairs! He lunged forward.

"There is no need to run, Liam." Another rush of sensation slammed into him. "You are coming with me."

"What?" Liam shouted above the blurring surge of colour. He scrambled to his feet, his hands scrabbling over the rough stone, feeling for a way out. "G-g-go…? Go where?"

"Lyskerrys of course." Iridescent blue - pulsing in time with his heart.

Liam edged away, hugging the wall. Somewhere amongst the light and colour was a sound. Did she... did she just laugh?

"I'm afraid you really have no choice Liam. You are going to have to trust me," Red. Deep, deep red, all spikes and sharp edges, pressing into his mind. "You do trust me, do you not?"

Like fuck he did! At best she was a bloody hallucination, and at worst... Then again... she hadn't actually harmed him, and now those crazy sensations were easing a bit and the light had calmed to a gentle lavender, it was actually quite... pleasant. Anyway, a vision couldn't hurt you. So yeah, maybe he did trust her, just a little. Although hadn't there been something going on a moment ago? Something... weird? It didn't seem very likely, not with Kerenza here. Yeah, he was pretty sure he knew her from... somewhere. She'd never let any harm come to him. There was nothing to worry about.

"Yeah, okay." Was that his voice? It did sound kind of like him, but Kerenza was right there in front of him and it was hard to think straight with someone as lovely as her... so... close. And her eyes... God they were beautiful. "Of course I'll come with you." Was that him too? Whoever it was sounded like they knew what they were doing, and it was better that having to think about it himself.

"Come Liam, it is time to leave for Lyskerrys."

Lyskerrys, that would be nice. Hadn't Jacob been there recently? It would be fine if JJ had been there.

"But how will we get there?"

"All you need to concern yourself with is not letting go of my hand," The scent of gardenias drifted through the chamber.

"Wait, what?"

Liam shuffled his feet, and water splashed over his shoes, soaking into the bottoms of his jeans. What now? He looked down. Water was seeping into the chamber, and it was rising fast.

CHAPTER 12

Many things were a mystery to The-man-who-didn't-know-who-he-was, but he knew he had a name. He even knew what it was because the woman that would occasionally come to visit him high in the forest city used it when she spoke to him. Perhaps people had more than one name, again, he couldn't remember. But the name she used felt comfortable and familiar, so he supposed that even if he did have different names, this was the one he must have used most.

Since he first found her waiting in the darkened house, the woman had visited many times. She was, without doubt, the loveliest creature he'd ever known. The man suspected that although there were probably many other people in the world, none could be as lovely as her. One truth shone a light through the darkness that was the man's memory, and that was that beauty comes from within. And the woman who came to visit glowed like the moon on a dark night.

There were a lot of things the man did not know, but he knew the woman. He knew how to make her smile, and what she really meant when she said one thing but meant something else.

One night when the scent of lilies drifted up to the forest city, The-man-who-didn't-know-who-he-was and The-loveliest-woman-in-the-world lay on their backs together on one of the footbridges high above the forest floor. They kicked their dangling legs idly back and forth over the edge of the walkway as they gazed up at the night sky.

"What's that one?" the man asked her, pointing to a group of stars.

"That's the Swordsmith." The woman took the man's hand in her own and pointed to the left of the constellation. "That group there is the hammer, that line of three stars with the little cross at the top is the blade, and that almost square shape there, can you see it? That's the anvil."

"And that one?" he asked, pointing to another spray of stars blazing between a pinwheeling galaxy and a blooming green nebula.

"That's the Wild Hunt. The brightest star, there, out in front of the others is Herla. And the most beautiful of them all, see it there at the back, the one that cannot decide which colour to be and so is all colours at once? That's Chastity."

"And who am I?" he asked turning his gaze away from the impossible beauty of the night sky to the impossible beauty of the woman next to him.

"That is something I wish I could tell you more than anything else," she replied. "It pains me to see you so lost, but unfortunately I don't know the answer to that question myself yet." It seemed like a reasonable response. If the man himself didn't know who he was, how could he expect anyone else to?

"Do that thing again," he said, "where you bring it to life."

The woman smiled and said, "I may not be able to give you the memories you crave, but at least I can give you that. Look back to the Swordsmith."

The-man-who-didn't-know-who-he-was turned his head to the constellation and smiled as the familiar sensation of magic-use began to build within him. High above them, a fine line of turquoise light followed the woman's outstretched arm and began to connect the stars together. It raced from one to another until the Swordsmith was drawn in exquisite detail across the sky. A flutter of excitement rippled along the man's back as the magic grew stronger. Then there was movement in the skies. The mighty Swordsmith brought his arm down, swinging the hammer in a sky-spanning arc across the night. It connected with the anvil in a shower of falling stars that exploded from the blade, plummeting earthwards to splash, sizzling and popping, into the pools and streams running across the forest floor.

The man smiled and closed his eyes, allowing the night to caress his skin. He may have no idea who he was before, but he knew who he was now. He was a part of this moment, and right now, nothing else mattered.

The-man-who-didn't-know-who-he-was and The-loveliest-woman-in-the-world lay for long hours and mere moments, watching galaxies revolve and the birth of stars and fireflies glow until finally the woman untangled her fingers from his. "I'm sorry, but I have to go now I'm afraid."

"I wish you didn't. It's lonely here without you," said The-man-who-didn't-know-who-he-was.

"I know," said The-loveliest-woman-in-the-world, "I wish I didn't too, but I will return soon."

CHAPTER 13

Liam spun around, looking wildly from side to side. Water flooded the chamber. Already, his feet were off the ground, and he was flung around and around by the spinning water. The dark walls and the sunlit stairwell flashed past. Dark, light, dark, light, dark, light. He tried to call out, but his words were lost in the roaring of the vortex. He tugged at Kerenza's hand; they had to get to the stairs, or they'd be forced up against the arched ceiling and drowned. Then everything went silent - he was under.

Twisting currents dragged him down. The floor was gone. The chamber was gone. The light rapidly dimmed until everything was black. Black and icy cold. Shivers spasmed through him as his body heat was sucked away. With Kerenza's hand clamped in his own, he could feel her spiralling away beneath him. His fingers loosened as his hands grew cold and unresponsive. Her hand slipped free. He thrashed out, stretching down into the darkness. There was a brush of fingertips, then another, and then she was gone.

He was lost, deep in black water, spinning and spinning and spinning. His lungs burned and screamed at him to take the breath that would kill him. Liam thrashed his head from side to side. Don't do it! Don't breathe!

His pulse banged in his head, in his chest, in his ears.

Don't take the breath.

God don't take the breath.

The breath.

Take the breath.

TAKE THE BREATH!

Liam gasped, dragging icy water deep into his lungs. Water flooded into every alveolus, but still his lungs screamed for relief and still his heart banged like thunder.

Soon his movements twitched to a halt. With the last of his strength, Liam thrashed out one last time for the surface. Nothing happened; the movement was all in his mind. It was already too late.

And in the end, it was nothing like it is in films; it was all lies. There was no hand reaching down through the water at the last second to save the drowning man. Sometimes all that happens is you run out of air in the dark: terrified and alone.

CHAPTER 14

The ground reared up, pivoted around and smashed into Liam's side. He sucked in a huge lungful of air and retched, wincing against the burning along his throat as he coughed the water from his lungs.

Except…

Except there was no water.

His chest still hurt like hell, but he'd take that over being dead any day.

Liam lay on his back waiting for the retching to subside and gasping between each new spasm. Christ, the air tasted good though. Believing you were dying certainly had a way of making you appreciate the simple things.

"Did I not tell you to keep hold of my hand? Humans! Come on, we have work to do."

He snapped his head up. Kerenza? Jesus, she had some nerve, standing there ordering him around like this was all perfectly normal. Liam propped himself groggily up on his elbows. "You might have warned me. I thought I was dying back there. I could've…" Wait, something wasn't right here.

He patted his trousers. They were bone dry. He'd been underwater, he should have been soaked through. He looked back to her. "Hang on a minute, just what the hell is…" But there was something else, something more that he should be getting. He was alive. He wasn't wet. But Kerenza was just standing there looking down at him as he lay on the ground. What was that all about? It was like she was waiting for him to notice something.

"Look, come on, enough's enough. What the actual…"

On the far bank of a wide river a child squealed in delight as her mother grabbed her around the waist and swung her away from the edge. "Keep away or the Morgen will get you!" The child laughed, squirming and wriggling in her mother's arms. They had to be twenty yards away or more, and yet he could hear every word. It was like they were right beside him. And their clothes, they looked almost… medieval.

"Look, where exactly are…"

Wait… the river… that was it! And the fountain behind them. That was what was wrong. The water blurred like wind-rippled silk. Like he was seeing the it both a fraction of a second before and after, well, now.

And it was lilac.

Kerenza glanced down her nose at him and tutted. "You will become used to it. Give it an hour and you will not even notice." He understood every word; the colours and smells that overwhelmed him at the well were gone.

But now he saw it, and it wasn't just the water either. It was everything. Everything was more intense, more real, more present. Liam drew in a long slow breath, and a heavy floral scent billowed through his mind. God, the colours… they were so brilliant, but there was more. It was like they blurred past the edge of the familiar spectrum.

Beyond the fountains. Beyond the graceful, organic buildings, there were mountains, pin-sharp through the soft summer haze.

He'd seen this before, when he'd followed Kerenza through the town, when the world had rippled around him, but this wasn't Liskeard. It wasn't even Cornwall. In fact, Liam was pretty sure it wasn't even his own world.

CHAPTER 15

"Do try and focus. I know this is all very new, but you need to stop and listen. It is important." Kerenza rolled her eyes. For the love of the Soul, why did these people always react this way? They were like children. They were worse than children. But it was important, really important, especially for him, if only he had the sense to see it. It would not be the first time someone from Tiranaral had become entranced by this place and ended up lost forever. Ordinarily she would have simply... well, you couldn't do everything for them, could you? But she could not allow that to happen to him. She had plans for Liam Verren.

"Sorry Kerenza. I'm listening, okay? I'm listening."

He wasn't. She could see that. Already his gaze was starting to drift away from her, and his mouth was dropping open again. They always did this, no matter how much you tried to tell them. It really was their own fault.

Kerenza grasped his shoulders, forcing him to look at her. She could beguile him of course, but then they just did as they were told, and later, when it wore off, she would be no further ahead than now. She shook him a little. He blinked and looked straight at her. Now, make him understand now, before he starts with all the worshipping and adoration. They always did that too.

"There is just one thing you need to remember. Can you do that? Remember one simple thing?" He nodded. "Very good. Time here is not like it is in your world; it moves differently. Stay here too long, and everything and everyone you love will be nothing but dust." A snap of her fingers drove the point home. "They will never understand you know. Their little lives will blink out, and they will die wondering why you abandoned them."

That got through. She let him feel it, just for a moment. Watched the despair form on his face. Who would have thought they could love a place like Tiranaral so much? She brushed her hand down the side of his face - so like children. It was almost a shame to put them through it, but it really was the only way; how else would they ever understand? She allowed the glamour drop away. He would be overwhelmed again in no time.

***

Liam gasped in a breath, tears burned his eyes, blurring his vision. They were dead, all of them! It wasn't even his world anymore. Then Kerenza was back. The devastation drifting through his head faded like a decaying nightmare. Jesus, did she do that? A half-smile played across Kerenza's lips. Liam backed away, stumbling and shaking his head, his mouth and eyes open wide in fear. She clucked and tutted at him.

"Get the fuck away from me, I mean it Kerenza! What the hell was that? What did you do to my head?"

"Do not take on so, it was just a little beguilement. Nothing you need to worry yourself about."

Just a little beguilement? More like some kind of… mind control. "Wait, back at the well… that was you too?"

Kerenza rolled her eyes. "Of course it was me. Who else would it have been? Certainly no one from Tiranaral."

She was annoyed. A disconcerting eddy of fear swirled through his thoughts. You had to be careful not to stay too long for... some reason or other. Liam wrapped his arms around himself and shuddered. The time thing, obviously, and... whatever. It felt like it might be a good idea not to upset her.

A splash caused him to jerk his head around. There was a brilliant flare of sunlight in the water of a fountain as a fish with fins of a colour that blurred far into the ultra-violet flopped back down into the water. It flicked in panic at some imagined terror and darted into the depths. Its long tail trailing behind it like an afterthought.

Liam dashed over to the water. "What the… that fish! Its tail, I… I don't even know the name of that colour! What do you call that?" And then he was looking at the sky and laughing. "Are those stars? But it's full daylight."

Kerenza's lips turned up in a half smile. "Am I to assume that you like it here in Lyskerrys?"

Lyskerrys? There was that name again. Bloody hell, he'd forgotten. Didn't she say something about Lyskerrys back at the Pipe Well? It was hard to remember— things had been pretty vague then. But if this was Lyskerrys… Christ! Jacob, he'd have to tell him! It would change everything! It was all real, everything his dad had said, it was all true. The divorce, the ridicule, the bullying, none of it needed to have happened.

But neither Jacob nor his dad could be the reason she'd brought him here and judging by the way she'd spoken to him since, she wasn't doing it for Liam's benefit either. There was one other possibility of course, the one where he'd wake up in a room with no sharp edges, pumped full of antipsychotic drugs. Still, if that was the case, he was probably already there, it might be best to just roll with it for now. He didn't have a whole lot of choice.

"Look, what's this all about Kerenza? I mean, don't get me wrong or anything, it's bloody amazing, but why? Why did you bring me here? It can't have been easy, or everyone'd be at it."

Kerenza was speaking again. "There have been certain recent... let us call them... developments, that mean we require the assistance of someone from Tiranaral."

"Tiranaral?"

"Your world."

"... and you chose me because?"

"Oh, that was the easy part," she said, waving the question away, "It had to be someone who had been here before."

CHAPTER 16

Vyvyan tore under the archway into the Chamber of the Soul. Behind her, footsteps and laughter echoed from the worn stone walls; Wenna and Jori were close. "Go on Wenna! You almost have her!" shouted Jori. Vyvyan shrieked and launched herself across the chamber, heading for the little dome that housed the Soul. A thrill of excitement tingled across her back as she twisted away from the hand on her shoulder that would end the game.

The touch never came.

Vyvyan stopped and gazed around. Everything in the chamber slowed and drifted to a halt: the people crowded around the dome, the birds lifting from its roof, the waterfalls running over it. Everything was frozen in time - everything except the Soul, which bathed the room in slow ribbons of light. What was happening? She had never seen anything like this before – never, ever. She was so surprised she almost forgot to breathe. Vyvyan drew in a deep breath, and in an instant, she was connected to everything. Everything, everywhere.

She was molten magma boiling through the skin of the world and rain falling on the high moors, as soft as a child's kiss.

She was the sharp focus of a lone buzzard circling in a rising current of warm air and the fear coursing through the veins of the small creature caught in its gaze.

She was the white-hot spark of recognition burning across the mind of the predator, and the cold charge of adrenaline surging through its prey.

She was the colour of lilies, the warmth of sunlight, the glorious night, and the crystal sea.

She was all these things and everything else, and she saw how the Soul touched them all.

When she breathed in again, Vyvyan was back in the chamber, and then everything happened at once: Wenna's hand clamped down onto her shoulder, a cloud of birds lifted squawking from the roof of the dome, and there was an explosion of sound as everyone resumed talking.

"Caught you!" proclaimed Wenna triumphantly, ploughing into Vyvyan's back and jolting her forward. Vyvyan stumbled a few steps, then stopped, staring ahead. Wenna stepped around in front of her, leaning in close to examine her face. "Vyvyan... are you... alright?"

Jori stamped to a halt next to Wenna. "What is wrong with her?"

Wenna poked Vyvyan's arm with a chubby finger. "I know not. She looks... funny."

Vyvyan blinked, and her mouth dropped open. She stared at Wenna and Jori with wide eyes. "I..." She covered her mouth with a small hand. She wanted to laugh. She wanted to cry. "I... I think I may be a Soul Breather."

***

Forcing back tears, Vyvyan straightened the river-pearl grips holding her silver hair in place, smoothed her robes, and raised her chin. The Soul might be gone, but she was High Priestess, and she had a reputation to maintain. She took the first step on the helical staircase that would lead her down to the Chamber of the Soul. Each time she came to the Cathedral now she was reminded of that first day when she was a child. Maybe it would have been easier to deal with then, but the years had slipped past, as years do.

Lyskerrys was almost certainly doomed of course. Her chest tightened at the thought, and fresh tears burned behind her eyes. She took a deep, shaking breath before taking another step down. There was only one hope left now. She prayed she had made the correct choice in sending Kerenza to recruit the Otherworlder; she could be somewhat... single-minded.

Vyvyan stepped down off the final step and onto the floor of the chamber, her stiff turquoise gown rustling as it slipped over the tread behind her. It was always worse when she reached the chamber. The Soul was gone. It was really gone. The light of all their lives had been extinguished. Little sparks of light flared and danced in front of her eyes. It was not usually this bad. She touched her fingers to her chest; her heart fluttered like it had forgotten its rhythm. The cavern began to spin around her, and she grasped the handrail for support. Her legs buckled, and she lowered herself to the steps.

The silence of the Cathedral was broken by a hollow metallic sound. In the main chamber, a younger woman dressed in the deep russet-brown of a timeliner, ignored the bowl she had dropped, and ran towards the staircase. "Vyvyan!" The bowl continued to ring as it rolled around on its rim on the flagstones, and candlelight glinted from her copper armbands and bracelets.

The timeliner knelt on the bottom step. "Vyvyan, are you okay?"

"Tamsyn?" Vyvyan blinked uncertainly, "Tamsyn. Yes, yes, I'm fine. There is no need to worry."

Tamsyn turned and sat on the step next to her, releasing a long slow breath. In her hurry to reach Vyvyan, a lock of hair had come loose and flopped over her face. She tucked it back under the band of ivy that circled her head. Vyvyan smiled; Tamsyn's hair did seem to have a will of its own.

Taking Vyvyan's hand in hers and placing the other protectively over the top, Tamsyn closed her eyes. Vyvyan glanced up, still smiling. "Are you checking up on me?" Tamsyn's violet eyes flashed open. The faint glow that had begun to infuse the bands spiralled around her arms, flowed rapidly away like frightened mice.

"No," she said in a voice that sounded very much like it meant yes. She flashed her disarming one-sided smile and continued. "Of course not, I would never be so presumptuous."

Vyvyan adored Tamsyn's company. Whereas certain other senior members of the Cathedral thought her disrespectful, Vyvyan found her irreverence refreshing. But whatever they thought, no one doubted Tamsyn's talents.

"Come on then, since you claim to be okay," said Tamsyn, pulling Vyvyan to her feet. "We have had news from Kerenza, she's on her way here now. While we wait, how about making yourself useful? You can help me clean up this mess."

Vyvyan allowed herself to be led through the Cathedral, smiling despite her worries. Tamsyn certainly had a way of lifting the spirits of those around her.

"Did the Otherworlder agree to help?" said Vyvyan.

"He did," replied Kerenza.

"And you told him everything?"

"I told him enough."

"Oh, did he seem afraid?"

"No, but when I told him he had been here before, he was quite reluctant to accept it."

"That is hardly a surprise though is it? The whole point of clouding their memories is precisely so they are unable to remember. But he must be fully informed Kerenza. Deceiving him will not help us."

"There was no deceit. I am telling him a little at a time. He will know everything eventually. Let Enys Avalen work its magic, he will be… keen to help."

"And his memory?"

"He is awaiting you at the Summer Court. You can restore it now."

"And do you think him capable?"

"Yes, I believe he is."

CHAPTER 17

"Jesus! What the hell was that?" Liam lurched to his feet and staggered backwards away from the couch, breathing heavily.

"I am sorry," said Vyvyan, "did Kerenza not warn you how a mind-to-mind contact would feel?"

Well, yeah, if describing it as *rather intimate* counted as a warning. Which, actually, it didn't. It wasn't even close.

"I should have asked her beguile you first, to ease the shock a little. Are you ready to try again?"

No bloody way was he ready to try again. Vyvyan's emotions had mixed with his until he couldn't tell them apart, and he knew her experience of him had been just as deep. There'd been something else there as well. Something slow and dark, and not fully… her.

"No, not really." Could you say that to a High Priestess? Vyvyan was the first he'd ever met; how the hell was *he* supposed to know?

Kerenza flicked a disinterested glance towards him, and in moments his thoughts took on a slippery, dreamlike quality. Wait, was he okay with that? Had he said he was okay? Perhaps he had. It did seem like something he would have said. Liam blinked and looked around. He was sitting down on the couch again beside Vyvyan. When, exactly, did that happen? Did he do that too?

Vyvyan leaned forwards and placed her hands back on his temples. Liam gritted his teeth; this was going to be uncomfortable. But then again, if he was to allow anyone access to his consciousness, he couldn't think of a better candidate than Vyvyan. Which was an odd thing to think, they'd only just met, but well, she was the High Priestess wasn't she? If you couldn't trust a High Priestess, who could you trust?

She was back in his mind again.

It was still a shock.

Instantly he was immersed in unfamiliar feelings; Vyvyan's emotions, but Christ, they felt like his. He loved the colour yellow because it felt like sunlight on his skin, wait, her skin. And the smell of rain - the way made her want to dance. Wave after wave of sensation, more and more intense. He was losing himself in what it was to be Vyvyan. He lived her life through her emotions. The soft, secure love she felt for her parents, the overwhelming sense of oneness and connection with everything that came from the Soul, a deep attachment to… not a daughter exactly, not even family, but close. On and on through her life, the joy and the heartache, he was with her, feeling it all. Until a final, sudden, wrenching loss. An awful, abyss, a void that could not be filled. Her tears flowed down his face. Christ, how could he have known?

"Vyvyan. Oh my God. I wasn't expecting… I didn't know…"

And then he couldn't speak anymore. Like a drop of blood in a glass of water, streamers and ribbons of experience coiled and unfurled through his mind. Slowly, a memory dispersed throughout his whole being. Like a broken dream, it was all there:

He blinks away the snow settling on his eyelashes. Jesus, it's cold. He stuffs his red, throbbing hands into his pockets, Ouch! What the hell is that? A blade bites into his palm. Travis' paper knife? But how did that… Something has changed, something about the night, something about time. A woman races out of the blizzard, lost and terrified in their own back garden. Celyn? The Hunt! The bloody Wild Hunt! An army of deranged, lightning-drunk freaks. Run, for Christ's sake… Travis, Evan, Celyn. Run!

Vyvyan's hands fell from his temples. She smiled apologetically.

Celyn. How could he ever have forgotten Celyn? The Lord of Misrule… The Knocker… The Solstice Blade…

Beside him, Vyvyan closed her eyes and slumped into the quilted back of the bench, "Intense, isn't it?"

Liam raised himself from the couch and walked slowly across the room. It was like he wasn't really there. He knew what beguilement felt like, and this wasn't it. Those were his memories. He'd always known… somewhere. But until now… Behind him urgent voices called his name, but they were… so far away. Only one thing mattered: Kerenza was right - he had been here before.

A boisterous chirping arose, broke through Liam's thoughts. The whole front of the Summer Court was like a sheet of rippled glass where a waterfall arced down from the top of the building. A flock of birds darted squabbling and twittering through the gap, occasionally dipping a wingtip into the rushing water. It didn't seem quite as unusual as when he'd first entered the room.

"Finally!" said Kerenza.

Liam turned back from the balcony. He'd forgotten she was even there; Vyvyan had been his whole world for more years than he'd even lived. "Do you understand now? You were touched by our world. There will always be a connection. Now, do you think we can get on?"

He could have done without the sarcasm, but she had a point; there was a connection. He had been cut by a Solstice Blade. Liam looked up, rubbing at the remembered pain in his palm, at the scar. "You beguiled me." It sounded petulant, even a little childish, but she hadn't even asked.

"Yes, well… you would have blocked it had you known. You humans cannot help yourselves."

But shouldn't that have been his choice? The beguilement had definitely been lifted. He wouldn't have questioned her a moment ago. Vyvyan placed her hand on his arm.

Kerenza glanced down disdainfully and tutted. "Provided our guest feels recovered enough, can we continue?"

Vyvyan flashed her a warning before returning her attention to Liam. "Do you know what a soul is Liam?"

"Yeah, I think so. It's your spirit; it's what makes you, well… you."

"Here in Enys Avalen, or the Otherworld as you call it, a soul has a physical presence. Every city has a soul. Unfortunately, the Soul of Lyskerrys has been…"

"The Soul is missing," interrupted Kerenza, "Without it Lyskerrys is dying - fading from the world. Soon it will be lost. You will never be able to return."

"What? It… but it can't be, I mean look at this place. It might feel like a dream, but it's all here, it's all real. How can it be dying?"

"Oh, it is not just Lyskerrys," Kerenza's eyes lingered on Vyvyan, "it is all of us. If Lyskerrys is lost, we all go with it."

"Wait, everyone? Even Vyvyan?"

Kerenza huffed and rolled her eyes. "Of course Vyvyan, what do you think *all of us* means? There is just one chance to save it, and that is you. I... we, I mean we. We simply cannot let you..."

"Kerenza." Vyvyan arched an eyebrow at the younger woman. For an instant, Kerenza's jaw tightened, then she lowered her eyes. Something felt wrong here. The situation was getting crazier by the second.

Liam looked from Vyvyan to Kerenza. "Christ, I'm sorry, but w-what do you think can I do about it?"

Kerenza drew in a slow breath. "Let me make this simple enough for even a human to understand. We believe the Soul to be in Tiranaral - in your world. It is… difficult for me to be there, but it is easy for you." She closed her eyes and pinched her brow. "You can come and go as you please, and you will not look out of place there. So, as ridiculous as it may sound, we need you to get it back for us."

Liam was on his feet. "Wait, wait, wait. Can we just slow down a bit? You've brought me here, beguiling me, because it was apparently too hard for you to communicate with me. Then you did it again because I couldn't let Vyvyan into my mind. Why are you even bothering to ask me? You'll just beguile me anyway. And I don't even know what it really is, this Soul. It's not like I'm going to just pop back and find it lying at the bus-stop or something."

Vyvyan stood and came to stand behind him, placing her hands on his shoulders. "Liam, there is no need to worry. You are not being forced into anything; the beguilement just stops you from panicking and making rash decisions. As for what the Soul is, it will appear to you as an aquamarine; a crystal about the size of an apple. But the Soul is much more than its physical presence - you experienced it when our minds were joined. And you are correct, in all probability it will not be out in plain sight, but we do have a way to lead you straight to it."

Kerenza stomped over, leaned in close, and hissed directly into Liam's ear. "I do not think you have grasped just how important this is. The loss of the Soul is associated with certain… additional —"

Vyvyan spun around. No longer an elderly woman; she was all High-Priestess. "Kerenza! That will do! You have other duties to attend to, do you not?"

Kerenza's eyes widened and her mouth dropped open. "Of course. As you wish High Priestess." She backed away a few paces with her eyes downcast, before turning and walking stiffly from the room.

"I apologise," said Vyvyan. "Truly. Kerenza is better informed that most and understands what the loss of the Soul means. Sometimes she… she's just worried. As are we all. For now, you must trust us. Everything will be made clear to you. But too much time has passed, and you need to get back to Tiranaral. Now, can you tell me where the gateway is?"

This was getting beyond silly. All these bizarre revelations, and manipulations and whatever the hell that thing between Kerenza and Vyvyan was just then, and now, bang, time to go home? "The gateway? No, how the hell would I know where the gateway is?"

Vyvyan leaned in and brushed a finger across his temple, and for a heartbeat the connection between them flared into life again. "Once again Liam. Do you know where the gateway is?"

No.

Wait...

Yes.

Yes, actually, he did know where it was, but he didn't know how. Slowly, Liam raised his eyes to Vyvyan's, his brow drawn down in confusion. "The f-fountain. The gateway's at the fountain."

Vyvyan smiled and squeezed his arm. "Very good. We call it Ventonana, or just The Ana, but yes, you are correct, the gateway is at the fountain."

CHAPTER 18

Liam flopped down onto his bed. Holy crap! It hadn't really hit him until he emerged from the pipe well; the sudden normalness and familiarity threw it all into stark relief. Jesus Christ, there was another world out there. Another bloody world! It didn't make any sense at all.

He'd tried to hide his feelings as he walked back to his flat, but he couldn't have made a very good job of it; people had started to look and mutter. Eventually, he'd given up and just run, leaving a wake of raised eyebrows and disgruntled comments behind him. Sod them - they could talk all they wanted; it wouldn't change anything. No wonder Jacob's dad had been so fired up.

Jacob! He had to tell him; it'd turn his life around. Unless… wasn't that exactly what his dad had done - come back from Lyskerrys all excited and ready to change the world? Now they didn't even talk. But this was different - of course it was - no one listens to their dad, but Liam… well, he was a mate, and that meant something. He grabbed his phone and tapped on Jacob's contact icon. It'd be fine, just so long as he broke the news to him slow and easy.

"Alright Liam, what's up?"

"Jesus H effing Christ! Jacob, you're not going to believe this." Okay, so much for taking it slow. Better concentrate on easy.

There was laughter from the other end of the phone. "Liam, calm down mate! What aren't I going to believe?"

Wait, breaking the news over the phone was no good. This should be done face to face.

"Nothing. Well yes, something. Everything man. Something big.

"Well, make your bloody mind up, it can't be both."

"Look, you busy? Wanna meet up?"

"Yeah, okay, but you'll have to come round here, I've got… someone coming over to… borrow something later."

"Well cancel it. Once you've heard what I've… wait, no you haven't – you're gaming, aren't you?"

Jacob laughed easily, without a hint of embarrassment. "Okay then, but you'll still have to come here. I'm… gaming."

"You won't be after what I've got to tell you mate. I'm heading over now. Do. Not. Move. I'll see you in five."

***

"Alright Liam?" said Jacob, turning away from the doorway and navigating his way back through the dingy shoe-strewn hallway of his flat. "See yourself in - team-deathmatch."

When Liam entered the sitting room, Jacob was already sitting on the sagging, old settee with a game controller in his hand. On the television screen in front of him a chaotic scene of carnage unfolded. The image rolled and twisted at dizzying speed as Jacob's fingers flew over the buttons on the controller.

How was he going to start this? He couldn't just come straight out with it. There was too much history. He'd have to build up to it. "Still sleepwalking?"

"What?" said Jacob, Sleepwalking? Who the fuck said anything about sleepwalking?"

Okay, so possibly not the best way to broach the subject. JJ clearly wasn't ready to come clean about that just yet. "Well, no one really. I just thought…"

Jacob lurched forward on the sofa. "Shit! Did you see that guy - camping in the bombed-out church? Bloody noobs!"

"What? Oh, Yeah, bloody... campers." Liam paced backwards and forwards across the front room. Jacob might be able to follow both the game and the conversation at the same time, but for crying out loud, this was important.

"JJ, could you pause it, just for a second?"

"Sorry mate, online game, I've got my stats to think about."

"Look, JJ, something's happened, something weird and I thought you should know about it."

"Yeah? Something like what?"

"You know last time I saw you - when we went to Java Joe's?" Jacob tensed. It wasn't much, but it was there. So there *was* something more to the sleepwalking thing. Liam continued; it'd have to wait. "Well, straight after that I went to the Pipe Well."

"The Pipe Well? What'd you wanna go to that dump for?"

"What? I didn't, not really, I was on the phone to Daisy, I just sort of ended up there. Look…"

Jacob swerved and ducked as he tried to dodge a hail of gunfire raining down from the roof of a building across the road.

Liam pressed on: "Once I got there, I…"

"Fuck! Fuck! Fucking snipers!" Jacob launched his controller across the room where it bounced off a chair before rattling across the kitchen floor. On the screen, his avatar performed an acrobatic pirouette and dropped to the ground.

On another display somewhere in the world a small notification announced that KernowBae23 had left the game.

"Okay," Jacob closed his eyes and blew out a long breath. "Okay, all good. Go on, you went down to the well..."

"So, once I got there…"

"Jesus, those guys fuck me off! Bloody campers."

Liam smiled, that was so Jacob. "That's when things started to get, I dunno, a bit weird. Wait, no, look before that I started having these odd dreams, about a week or so ago, I suppose."

Jacob grinned "Oh great! I just love hearing about other people's dreams. You do know they aren't real, right? And do you think you could you stop pacing? You'll wear out the bloody carpet."

Liam walked over to a chair, sat down then immediately jumped up again. Oh, Jacob was *so* going to wish he'd been paying attention in a minute! "The night of your dust up with Davy and Beckerleg, I wake up with the name Kerenza in my head and then I hear voices, raised voices outside, and I go to investigate, but then, before I get there, I see someone in the street. It's crazy, but it's her, Kerenza - from the dream - but then she isn't there anymore, so I've imagined it, right? Anyway, Monday morning I'm on the bus and there she is again, and she wants me to follow her, and... I try, but I... lose her. Then on Saturday, just after I leave you, she appears again, so I follow her to the Pipe Well only this time she doesn't disappear."

"Whoa, what the hell mate? Are you... okay? Think about what you're saying man - seriously. It sounds like you're off your head."

"What? JJ listen, I..."

Jacob was almost pulling himself back into the sofa and looking at Liam like he had a disease he could catch. Crap this hadn't been such a good idea after all.

Liam stepped back, holding out his hands, he *had* been crowding Jacob a bit. He probably just needed some space. "JJ, okay, okay. Look, it's not like it sounds, I'm okay."

Liam took a deep breath. "I tried to talk to her, and that was when things got really strange." Great, he really should have thought this through. "She spoke, but the words got all mixed up with colours and tastes and feelings."

Jacob pulled his feet up from the floor. "Yeah? It doesn't sound okay to me. It sounds like an acid trip."

"Yeah, well it's not," Liam snapped. "You know I'm not into that crap." Christ, he'd come here to try and help, the least Jacob could do was hear him out.

Jacob looked up at Liam. "Okay, I know, I know. But you were clearly hallucinating. Could anyone have given you something without you knowing? Spiked your drink or something?"

"No. No way. I didn't see anyone or go anywhere else. I was at home asleep all night. And anyway, who would do that?"

"Well, in that case you need to go and see a doctor."

"Look, let me finish, will you? I wasn't drugged, and I don't need a doctor, okay?" It sounded quite convincing when he said it out loud; it was shame he didn't believe it himself.

"Okay, get on with it then."

"Alright, long story short. The water from the well spun up like a whirlpool, and we were sort of sucked down into it, and before you say anything, yes, I am well aware that it sounds freaking nuts, but when it stopped, I was somewhere else."

Liam closed his eyes and took another breath. *Here we go…*

"Jacob… It was Lyskerrys."

CHAPTER 19

"Lyskerrys? Are you fucking joking?"

"Whoa, JJ, hang on a second, let me explain."

Jacob looked away. His mouth clamped shut. "Because if you're trying to be funny, you're making a seriously bad job of it. Are you actually trying to piss me off, or are you just a lot more stupid than I thought?"

Christ, okay, so Liam had expected a bit of resistance, but this, really? Jacob was acting like a total twat. "Look, I know it sounds crazy, and it's dragging up all that stuff about your dad, but it's real, I was there."

Jacob's eyes flashed anger. "You need to go, and while you're at it, go and see a bloody doctor."

"Come on JJ, we're mates, aren't we? You're pissed off, I get it. But don't be an idiot. Think about it, all the bad stuff, the divorce, none of it needed to happen."

"Don't. You. Fucking. Dare."

"But Lyskerrys, it's..."

Bellowing, Jacob launched himself across the room, barging the coffee table aside, and sending a plastic chair spinning across the floor. He slammed into Liam, and the two of them careened backwards into a wall. Jacob swung a wild punch. Liam saw it coming and ducked, narrowly avoiding it.

"JJ, for Christ's sake man!"

The next punch didn't miss, cracking into Liam's jaw and snapping his head backwards. The impact spun Liam around, driving his head into the wall. Plasterboard cracked and sunk.

Jacob stepped back, eyes wide staring down at his shaking hands. He slumped down onto the sofa. "Shit. Liam… I…"

"Fuck off Jacob. You want to deny everything? Fine. I was trying to help you. Remember that if you ever come to your senses."

Liam slammed the door to Jacob's flat behind him. He felt numb. They'd had their fair share of disputes over the years, but nothing like this. Rubbing his jaw, he turned and walked away.

CHAPTER 20

Liam touched his jaw gingerly and grimaced. He had come full circle and was now pissed off with Jacob again. In a couple more minutes he'd probably be back to blaming himself. Surely even Jacob must be able to see Liam was only trying to help. What other reason could he possibly have had for telling him? Talk about an over-reaction; sometimes Jacob could be a total arse.

Screw him. It didn't matter what Jacob thought, it wouldn't make Lyskerrys any less real. Although Liam doubted himself for a while after returning home. Afterall, dream-women appearing and then disappearing in the town, gateways to alternate realities. It wouldn't be too much of a stretch to suspect some kind of 'episode'. But now he was back in Enys Avalen, for the second time. So, yeah, he was pretty sure it was real.

"Liam!" Kerenza snapped.

"Sorry, what?"

"I told you to sit."

He dropped heavily into one of the lavishly upholstered chairs. He could do without Kerenza's attitude on top of everything else. "Sorry. I've got a few things going on right now. You're not the only one with problems, you know"

"Well, I would really rather you weren't so… preoccupied. I need you to concentrate."

When they'd entered the Summer Court, the walls in the front rooms danced with warm orange light, as the evening sun sparkled through the waterfall tumbling down the face of the building. But in the back, up on the second floor, darkness had already taken hold. Liam watched distractedly as Kerenza moved swiftly from candle to candle, lighting each one.

Thinking about it, Jacob was being more than just a bit of an arse. Of all the people he could have spoken to, Liam would have chosen Jacob anyway. They'd always shared everything. What a twat! Back when all that stuff with his dad first started, Liam had always stood by him. He brushed his fingers along the side of his face, and sharp, hot pain throbbed through his jaw. Some bloody way to repay his support that was.

An irritated tapping caused him to look up. His mind had been wandering again. Kerenza had finished with the candles, and she didn't look impressed. She drummed her fingernails against the arm of her chair, her mouth a thin, tight line.

"Sorry. I'm fine, honest." And then there was Kerenza. She was only interested in what he could do for her. There hadn't been a whole lot of appreciation so far.

"Remember Vyvyan told you we had a way to lead you straight to the Soul?" Kerenza began. "Well, just before it was taken…"

"What? You said it was missing, no one said anything about it being taken."

"Taken or lost, it matters not. The result is the same, the Soul is gone, and we have to get it back."

"Well actually, it kind of does matter, since it's me you're expecting to go after it." Each time Kerenza spoke to him, there was something else she had conveniently forgotten to mention. "No. You're asking me to trail a thief. You obviously don't know who it is. How do I know he's not dangerous?"

"Actually," said Kerenza, "how do you know that he is not, in fact, a she?"

"That's hardly the point is it?"

"Listen, whoever took it employed stealth. They clearly attempted to avoid confrontation. You are not going to engage with them, you are simply to locate the Soul."

"Kerenza. Are you even listening to me? I said no."

"Oh, hush now," she cooed, "you only think like that because this is all new to you. There really is nothing to worry about."

Maybe she was right, and it did sound rather intriguing. He could at least hear her out, it wasn't like he was actually agreeing to anything yet.

"There is someone you will need to meet. She is in charge of the plan and will explain everything to you, then you will understand."

Then you will understand? Liam's eyes flicked up to Kerenza's. Did she just beguile him again?

That was when he noticed her eyes.

As they had been talking, the room had continued to darken, and now the only light came from the candles that Kerenza lit earlier. What was strange was how her eyes had faded to a soft green. "Does that always happen? Your eyes I mean, do they always change colour like that at night?"

Kerenza snapped her head up. "What?" she demanded. "What do you mean *change colour*?"

Christ, what now? First Jacob and now Kerenza. If he carried on at this rate, there'd be no one left in either world he hadn't pissed off. "Nothing, really, it's nothing. I didn't mean anything by it. Look, I'm sorry, okay?"

"Liam listen very carefully. This is important. Tell me - change colour how?"

"They... they just look softer in this light; the colour isn't as intense."

Kerenza tensed, and she peered around the room like she was searching for something. Liam followed where she looked, but nothing seemed out of place. Leaning forward until her face was just inches away from his own, she grasped each of his shoulders. "Look again. Is it the light, or is there is actually less colour in my eyes?"

"What?" She was so close. His heartbeat pounded in his ears. She was worried about something, frightened even, and if someone like her was scared... a prickling shiver ran down his back. He risked a glance back over his shoulder. "Does it matter?"

"It matters! "Look at my eyes!"

There was no mistake. "Colour," he blurted out. "It's the colour, it's not the light. Your eyes, they definitely aren't as green as they were earlier. I'm sure of it."

Kerenza grabbed him by the wrist and hauled him from the chair. He stumbled to his feet. What the hell was happening? And where was the Door? Light from the hallway had been glowing through it just moments before. He banged into something, and it skittered forward, toppling over. He grabbed at it before it fell; the back of a chair. It was right there in front of him! Why hadn't he seen it? Terror seeped through his mind, dark and viscous like a slowly spreading pool of blood.

Snap.

Snap, snap, snap.

What the hell was that?

Snap, snap.

Liam strained his eyes against the dark, but there was nothing there. He should've been able to see something. It was affecting his eyes, wherever he looked the light and colour drained away. Snap, snap-snap-snap-snap. There was something else in that bloody noise, it was like... were those words? It was repeating something, almost like it was saying... no, it couldn't be! "Oh shiiit! Kerenza – we've got to get the hell out of here. Now!"

Kerenza's fingers bit deep into his arm. She barrelled across the room, scattering furniture, and dragging him behind. Snap, snap, snapsnapsnap. Claustrophobia slammed doors shut in his mind. All he could do was run.

With one last violent tug on his arm, Kerenza jerked Liam through the door and flung him into the hallway. Pivoting around, she kicked the door shut behind them.

Momentum carried Liam across the hallway and slammed him into the opposite wall. The impact knocked the breath from his lungs, but it also broke the hold the events in the back room had over him. He threw his weight against the door as she spun the key in the lock.

"Come on!" she screamed, grabbing his arm, and running along the corridor. "A locked door will not hold it!"

They raced along the hallway, and out across the central atrium. Kerenza reached the other side first, madly rattling the handle of the closed doors; they were jammed. Turning his shoulder forward as he closed in, Liam slammed into them. He burst through in a shower of splintered wood, and fell, rolling, across the floor. He scrambled to get up, slipping on polished marble. "Wait!" said Kerenza, "Wait, it has gone. Look, the colour has returned."

"What?" replied Liam between laboured breaths. "Gone? As simple as that? Are you mad?"

CHAPTER 21

Rolling clouds of phosphorescence stirred up by the waterfall glowed deep within the Summer Court plunge pool. In the twilight the soft greens and lilacs were as unnaturally vivid as ever. It all seemed so… so peaceful.

Liam twisted round on the bench, glancing nervously back over his shoulder. He pulled his arms in tighter around himself. Beside him, Kerenza sat with her arms crossed, drumming the fingers of one hand against her arm. Her jaw was clenched closed.

"So," said Liam, "were you planning on telling me what the hell that thing was?"

"What?" Kerenza tutted, "Oh, for the Soul's sake, it matters not, it has gone now."

"That's it? It's gone? It was in the Court Kerenza! It scared the living crap out of me. If you hadn't dragged me out of there, I could've been…"

Kerenza spun around to face him, her eyes flashing. "Really? And what exactly would you know about it? Do you not think that I have might have more important things to worry about than how you are feeling?"

Liam bridled. "Now wait a bloody minute, I'm the one helping you out here! That thing knew my name! I'm more than a little freaked out to be honest, so don't give me..."

Kerenza grasped Liam's upper arms. "Wait, wait - it knew your name?"

Her face was white, this didn't look good. Liam glanced back over his shoulder again. "Y-yeah, I m-mean I wasn't sure at first, but, yeah, it definitely said my name. Christ, Kerenza, what the hell's going on?"

A little of the hardness left her face. "Yes, well. It is... regrettable that I did not have the chance to prepare you before you encountered it yourself. But I'm afraid that this is something new."

A light mist blew across the pool from the waterfall, raising goose-bumps on Kerenza's exposed shoulders. Liam's breath caught in his throat. God she was lovely, even when she was angry. Had he really never noticed that before? A stray strand of copper hair wavered across her face. It felt like they'd been talking about something - maybe a moment or two ago. It couldn't have been anything important though. Certainly not as important as the curve of her neck where it transitioned into her shoulder or the slight fluttering of her heartbeat pulsing at her wrist. A musician should see that, they could write a whole symphony around it. But those goose-bumps, she must be cold, and more than anything else in the world, Liam wanted to warm her chilled skin.

He blinked away the beguilement. Bloody hell, that was quick! They *had* been talking about something. He'd been angry with her about being kept in the dark about that thing in the court and then, suddenly... this.

"I know what you're doing," he said.

Kerenza rolled her eyes. The glamour lifted.

Movement on the far side of the pool made Liam look up. Vyvyan hurried around the path towards them, the hem of her aquamarine gown looped over her arm to keep it clear of her feet. "Liam, Kerenza," she panted when she reached them. "I just heard. Thank the Soul you are both alright. Was it…?"

Just then Liam's hair flicked up as something brushed past his head before arcing out across the water. Out over the pool, a bird skimmed the surface, dipping its beak into the water, cutting a perfect line through the uneven surface.

Vyvyan followed his gaze. "Twilight swallow," she said without looking back at him. "They only sing on the last day of their lives. It is said that it is the most beautiful sound you will ever hear. But it is a bad omen, a portent of death."

Perhaps informing him of the everyday details of Lyskerrys helped her deal with the dangers her city faced. Perhaps it was a warning about what they had experienced in the Court.

"So," prompted Liam, "that thing in the Court, you know what it was?"

Vyvyan paused, biting her lower lip as if reluctant to continue. "When we mentioned that we had other problems in addition to the Soul being lost, this is what we were talking about. We are not totally sure, but, well, we think it is a ghost." She raised her eyes to Kerenza. "You really should have been told." Kerenza looked away.

"A ghost? But…" A thousand reasons why it would be ridiculous to believe it was a ghost, crowded into his mind. But it was pointless. He knew that there were no such things as ghosts with the same certainty he knew you couldn't be transported through a six-inch-deep pool of spring water into another world. Whatever had pursued them through the Summer Court couldn't be a ghost, yet clearly, it was. "A ghost, but what does it want? Why is it here?"

Vyvyan leaned down and trailed her hand through the water. The action seemed to calm her, smoothing out the furrows in her forehead. "I am afraid I cannot answer your questions Liam." Below the surface, a glassy fish, with a flowing green and turquoise tail, caressed and rolled past her hand. She curled her fingers gently around its tail allowing it to brush through before it swam back out towards the tumult at the centre of the pool again. "Why is it here? We do not know. Its appearances are random but are becoming more frequent. Wherever it has been things are decaying and breaking down, and without the Soul, the city cannot heal. We simply do not know how much time we have left. About the only thing we can be sure of is that it almost always targets the gateways to your world."

"Actually," said Kerenza, "from what the human has just told me, that is not strictly true. We may have bigger problems."

CHAPTER 22

"It destroys everything it touches, but it seems to be particularly attracted to places with connections to other worlds," said Vyvyan as she and Liam walked up the incline towards the Ventonana. "Without the Soul, the city is unable to heal itself of the damage the ghost inflicts on it. It cannot be seen so easily here. It is much worse in places that have experienced a lot of hauntings. You will understand better if you see it for yourself."

At the highest point of a bridge arching over the Ebronndir, Vyvyan stopped and gazed out across the city. The fading daylight reflected from the waterways, and bright splashes of phosphorescence marked the positions of the fountains. A soft rushing sound heralded the arrival of a small flock of twilight swallows, flicking and rolling past on their way to roost. In the darkening skies above them, galaxies unfurled like flowers. It was hard to believe anything was wrong.

Vyvyan's eyes glistened. Liam stepped in close behind her and curled an arm across her chest. Her pain was his; he could still feel it. The connection lingered on in their shared emotions. This was her whole world, everything she had ever known. He shouldn't be able to understand, all he'd done was show up and be overawed by the beauty, but he could. He experienced every heart-wrench, every ache with her. But Vyvyan, all of them, lived it every day.

"I could not bear to lose it. Lyskerrys I mean." Her voice wavered, and Liam tightened his embrace. "This is why we need you, all of this, not just for me or any one of us. We cannot let Lyskerrys become just another lost city."

"Lost city?" he stumbled over the words, faltering as though she had spoken them. "Is that what Kerenza meant when she said it was fading?"

"Yes, there are other cities where this has happened, where the Soul has gone. They just start to fade, becoming harder and harder for outsiders to find until eventually, one day, no one goes there anymore."

"Fade? Like disappear?"

"Not in the visual sense as you understand it. Once the Soul has gone from a place it begins to recede from the world, becoming harder and harder for outsiders to find. Eventually they are only occasionally encountered by accident and those that do happen upon them often do not return. Then one day they are… lost. Do not let that happen to Lyskerrys."

He had to help, how could he not? This was no beguilement. It was like with dreams; you didn't know when you were beguiled, but you damned sure knew when you weren't. "Vyvyan, look, don't worry. I'll do what I can - anything. You need me to chase down a thief across worlds? Nothing to it, right?"

"Thank you, Liam," she said. "Really."

God, it must be so hard for her; keeping this up. How long had she endured this on her own? She patted his forearm where it lay across her chest and pulled away. "Come on."

Soon, the river fell behind them, and as the day faded, low lamps began to light up on either side of the path. The night draped over them muting the distant sounds of life as they moved further away from the city. Ahead, at the junction of two roads, stood another of Lyskerrys's fantastic fountains. Shadow covered one side of it. Shit, the ghost, was it back? No, it was just the lamps, some of them weren't working. Was this another sign of Lyskerrys failing?

"Can you see it?" Vyvyan stopped at the foot of the fountain.

"Yeah, the lamps, they're broken… or something."

"Yes, but there is more. Look closer."

Liam leaned in nearer to the fountain. Some of the shadows were in places that were still illuminated. "Oh yeah, now I see it. It's the stone, it's discoloured."

"It is worse than it looks. This way." At the rear of the fountain, dark stains spread across the stonework. Fingers and tendrils of corruption reached through the stone to the highest parts.

Liam gagged, as a sickly, sweet, stench caught in his nostrils. "Okay, it's not nice, but it's like some kind of mould isn't it? Some of the walls in my flat have it, admittedly it doesn't smell quite this bad, but you can just wipe it off."

Vyvyan placed a hand on the corner of the structure. Christ! The stone rippled - an obscenely slow undulation under her touch - like a paper-thin skin over something with much less solidity.

"Whoa!" Liam stumbled backwards in revulsion. "What the hell was that?"

But Vyvyan hadn't finished. She tightened her grip on the stone and pulled her hand away. A section sloughed off, sliding easily away from the rest of the stonework, trailing long threads of a dark, viscous, brown. Liam looked on appalled. The hole left behind gaped like a wound, oozing a thick, sticky substance like honeycomb left in the air for too long.

Vyvyan turned to face him. "I think that is enough for one visit. It is time for you to return to Tiranaral. You have been here far longer than you think. Do not forget that time will be magnified in your world."

She was right. When he had first emerged from the channel at the base of The Ana it had been daylight. Liam looked up; the sun had long since set, and the spiral arm of the galaxy now blazed across the dark sky. How could he have missed it? He'd noticed the light fading of course, but here, in Lyskerrys, it didn't seem to matter. It was too easy to forget that he had another life in another place.

He closed his eyes for a moment. In his mind, the gateway spat and fizzed at the front of the fountain. "Does it matter?" he asked. "That the gateway is affected by the decay?"

"If the decay is allowed to continue the gateway will close," replied Vyvyan. "But you will be perfectly safe for now."

"But what about the damage?" It felt like vandalism, just walking away and leaving it.

"There is nothing we can do," said Vyvyan. "The decay was already there, we just uncovered it. It will try to heal, but it will not succeed, not without the Soul."

"And what about coming back? I have to work during the week." It felt strange talking about work, here.

"A week? Well, that is longer than I would like, but you are correct, you must attend to your commitments in Tiranaral. Return when you can. Then go straight to the Cathedral and ask for me. Someone will be there even if I am not. They will summon me.

She led the way to the front of the fountain. "Put your hand into the water, you know how to use it now, the channel will pull you in and take you. It may seem strange once you are in, it is a different entrance. The important thing is not to panic. Remember that you know what you are doing and feel your way back to Tiranaral. Trust your instincts."

He hadn't worried about using a different channel, not until she just mentioned it. He was worried now, but he had no choice; time was passing. He needed to return home.

Reaching out to where a carved fish's head ejected a gentle arc of water, Liam placed his hand into the flow.

CHAPTER 23

Many things were a mystery to The-man-who-didn't-know-who-he-was, but he knew that the magic in the forest city was failing. He knew this because The-loveliest-woman-in-the-world had once taken him to a secluded glade deep in the sacred heart of the forest. There she had shown him magic that was so incredible that he could not see how anything could ever be more enchanting.

There had been no indication they were about to enter the glade, if anything, the trees and the undergrowth had become thicker and more difficult to navigate. The-man-who-didn't-know-who-he-was stumbled and tripped as his feet caught under tree roots while brambles snagged and pulled at his clothing. It was as if the forest didn't want them to progress any further. What little light filtered through the canopy became even more gloomy. Eventually, even the bird song and the sound of the wind in the leaves faded into silence. But still the woman led him on, deeper and deeper into the forest.

And then, after turning his back to the undergrowth to protect his face and forcing his way backwards through a bush one last time, they were there.

The meadow was filled with flowers, and insects buzzed and danced in the sunlight. The-man-who-didn't-know-who-he-was had to shield his eyes against the glare for a few moments after the darkness of the forest. Crossing their path ahead of them a stream of lilac water gurgled over rocks to empty into a pool in the centre of the glade. As he walked with The-loveliest-woman-in-the-world to the edge of the pool, the familiar sensation of magic built up inside him.

Next to the pool, and covered with brilliant green moss, was a circular stone platform. Weathered lines and symbols crossed and divided its surface, but their detail and meaning were long since lost to erosion.

The man knelt and ran his fingers over the velvet moss, tracing a line across its surface and wondering at its meaning. When he had reached as far as he could, he followed the line with his eyes. Then he froze and just stared. On the other side of the clearing stood a magnificent stag. It was easily as tall as he was at its shoulders, and the top of its crown of antlers was just as high again. The man gasped.

The woman told him to pay it no mind and go and stand in the centre of the platform. Then she told him to close his eyes.

In an instant he breathed in the whole world, and when he breathed out again, he was connected to everything everywhere. Overwhelmed, the man stepped backwards in surprise. His awareness was making connections, jumping from one thing to another.

He was the sunlight slanting through the trees, and the dancing motes of dust caught in the beams.

He was the rolling and splashing of the stream and the bubbles of oxygen it stirred up.

And he was the sound of the summer, just on the edge of hearing and the breeze through the meadow.

He was the green of chlorophyll in a million plants. And the iridescence of ten thousand insects. And red, red haemoglobin surging through a thousand tiny hearts hiding in the grass.

And finally, he was the mind of a stag, staring back across the meadow at a man with no memory.

At first the man was confused and more than a little scared, but the stag assured him there was nothing to fear. And he knew the stag was right, for it was his mind too. They were one and the same - a single consciousness in one body. He snorted and tossed his head to one side, laughing as he sensed the familiar weight of the rack of antlers. A sensation he had both never known and always known. The fierce joy of belonging so completely to this place propelled him forward, and he sprang away across the clearing.

Thundering across the meadow was pure exhilaration. At the far side he turned and raced back across the glade. Who had made that choice? Was it the man? Was it the stag? Did it even matter? The whistle and pull of the wind rushing through the stag's antlers, the pounding of its hooves, the pounding of his heart. These were timeless sensations that always had been, and always would be. The pool drew nearer, closer and closer, wider, deeper, until the stag leaped once again into the air and crossed it in a single bound.

At some point the man forgot that he had ever been a man and was simply one with the stag, racing and crashing through the forest.

Later, when he had returned to the pool and was once again a man who didn't know who he was, he was left with half-memories. The ruins of a dream in which he had stood at the top of a high hill, calling out across the land below - his land - tossing his antlers in a challenge to the world.

That was the first time the man had visited the glade, back when the magic was still working properly. He knew the magic was failing on his second visit. For one thing, the glade was not nearly so difficult to find, and when the stag came to him, he had been unable to fully enter its mind. The stag charged off across the clearing, but the man struggled to stay with it. It felt more like he was riding on the stag's back, fighting to stay mounted. Eventually, as the stag reached the edge of the meadow, He began to fall behind. Soon he was a man again, standing at the clearing's edge, watching the animal run off without him.

One day, in another part of the forest city, the-loveliest-woman-in-the-world encouraged the man close to edge of a platform. The nearer he got, the more buoyant he began to feel. It was like the air was full of unseen bubbles, surging up from the forest floor. With each step, the man struggled to keep his feet down more and more, until on his final attempt, he simply rolled and tumbled out into the air. Giddy and breathless, he bobbed and laughed in the space between the trees until the-loveliest-woman-in-the-world sailed out across the gap to him, laughing uncontrollably.

On his next visit, the rising stream of bubbles felt weaker. The man edged cautiously closer to the drop one foot at a time. Finally, he stepped out, but only a short way from the edge he began to sink into the air. The man flailed and grasped for the platform as it rose away from him. Although he fell slowly, there was nothing he could do to prevent his eventual landing in a deep, clear pool.

CHAPTER 24

Abruptly, the emptiness beneath his feet solidified, and Liam staggered sideways. For an endless moment he teetered on the edge of the steppingstone. "Shiiiit!" Pinwheeling his arms uselessly, he toppled sideways into the Ventonana pool.

Liam surged to his feet in a plume of lilac water, to gasps of surprise and laughter from a recently acquired crowd of onlookers on the bank. Heat flushed into his cheeks. Crap, not the best of arrivals. Brushing past a couple of ultraviolet-tailed fish, he pushed through the waist-deep water towards the edge of the pool.

A hand reached down from the crowd, grasped him just above the wrist, and began to pull. Liam squinted at the sunlight flaring from copper bands coiled around the owner's arms. Suddenly the grip loosened as the face beyond lost its composure and broke into fits of laughter. Liam fell backwards into the pool again, framed, for just a moment, by a fan of displaced water.

"Sorry," spluttered the woman. "Really, but you just look so ridiculous!"

Liam shook his head, smiling through his embarrassment. "Yeah, thanks, I got that."

Towards the back of the gathering crowd there was movement. "Come on now, move aside, let the poor man get out, and dry off." Smiling, Liam recognised Vyvyan. She stopped short of drawing him into an embrace, planting a kiss on his cheek instead as she made a show of avoiding his wet clothes. He laughed. It was hard to believe this was only their second meeting. Taking his hand, Vyvyan led him towards the entrance to the Cathedral. "It is so good to see you again Liam. Come, let us find you some dry clothes, and after that, there is someone you need to meet."

Liam shrugged the unfamiliar cream-coloured robes into a more comfortable position, setting unexpected air currents into motion around his upper thighs. It wasn't entirely unpleasant. Vyvyan adjusted the knotted, corded belt around his waist before standing back to admire the effect. "Neophyte's robes," she said. "We have lots of spares. You would be surprised how common misjudged landings are. Okay, I think you are ready. Come and meet Tamsyn."

"Tamsyn, is she the one with the plan for getting the Soul back?"

"It is rather more than just a plan. She is probably our most talented timeliner. You will be in very safe hands."

"Timeliner? What's a timeliner?"

"Come now, Liam. This is really no time for jokes," said Vyvyan. "You are familiar with our timeliners, are you not - those who are sensitive to the time differences between worlds?"

"Okay, if you say so," said Liam, "and we'd be needing one of those because…?"

Vyvyan's brow creased. "How else do you think we are to retrieve the Soul? It is already too late; the Soul is already lost."

"Sorry, Vyvyan, I literally have no clue what you're talking about." The way she looked at him was a bit of a worry; part confusion with a trace of panic.

"Oh, my word!" she said. "You really do not know, do you? Kerenza never told you!"

"Time-travel?" said Liam, "You've got to be joking. Time-travel? On top of everything else? For crying out loud Vyvyan."

"I am truly sorry Liam, but I can assure you that this is no joke. Kerenza really should have mentioned this to you before now."

Kerenza. No shit! Add it to the probably one million and one other things she really *should have mentioned* before now. But time-travel? Christ, there was so much that could go wrong. Bloody hell, he must be completely expendable. Kerenza was starting to seriously piss him off.

Liam felt the tension in Vyvyan's body before he saw her knuckles whiten against the handrail as they descended the helical staircase. He'd been so preoccupied trying to work through Kerenza's latest omission that he hadn't been paying much attention. "Vyvyan, what's wrong? Is everything okay?" For a moment he was back with her in the Summer Court, sharing her emotions again. Was this the slow, dark thing he caught a glimpse of when she'd cleared the blocks in his mind?

She rubbed his arm, and Liam drew in a relieved breath. Bloody hell, he could have done without that little shock, on top of the time-travel thing. "Yes, yes, I am fine. You have no need to worry. It is because the Soul is lost. We all feel it, but each time I return here it is somehow worse than I was expecting. Give me a moment, and I will be okay"

But she didn't look okay, as she closed her eyes, and inhaled a sharp breath. After a few moments she looked up. "Okay, let us continue."

The Cathedral was cavernous. Liam craned his neck looking up at the ceiling arching away into darkness. Smaller alcove rooms were arrayed around the edge at regular intervals, curtained off from the main chamber. Somewhere in the vaulted dimness above him birdsong echoed. It was certainly impressive, and probably would have been even more so if Liam hadn't been trying to process the idea of time-travel when he first encountered it.

The centre of the room was empty but for a white marble cupola surrounded by shallow moat. Channels carved into the floor ran towards it. Underneath the dome Kerenza was engaged in quiet conversation with another woman dressed in russet satin. Right at that moment, seeing Kerenza standing there, Liam didn't care how important she was, and Otherworld mind control notwithstanding, he had a few things he'd like to say to her. Time-travel currently being right at the top of the list. He didn't get the opportunity, as Vyvyan's next step caused her to stumble. Liam still had hold of her elbow, and supported her, but instantly, Kerenza turned and hurried towards them. In the silence, the clacking of her sandals echoed loudly. Her companion raced after her.

Reaching Vyvyan, Kerenza's eyes widened as she embraced the older woman. "You feel so thin. Is there nothing I can do?"

"Everything is as it should be Kerenza. Of all people, you know this," Vyvyan reassured her.

Linking her arm through Vyvyan's, Kerenza guided her to one of the benches around the edge of the pool. The woman in the russet satin arranged a pile of cushions and helped her to sit. Liam was left standing a little way away as the two women attended to Vyvyan. He pushed the thoughts of remonstrating with Kerenza to the back of his mind. They were clearly worried about her; his annoyance would have to wait. Was Vyvyan's condition really all due to the Soul being lost? Because they were acting like something else was seriously wrong. It was like there was something he wasn't being told. Vyvyan said they all felt this way, but Kerenza and her companion, didn't seem to be displaying any ill effects. Then again Vyvyan was High Priestesses, perhaps it was different for her.

Kerenza's voice interrupted his thoughts. "Come and join us Liam. This is Tamsyn, the one I told you about."

Tamsyn looked up with wide violet eyes. A lock of chestnut hair had come loose from the band of ivy encircling her head. She tucked it back. "Hello again. So, you are the mysterious Liam, are you? I've heard a lot about you."

"You?" Great, that was all he needed. It was her; the woman who had pulled him out of the pool earlier. Her opinion of him was probably already wavering somewhere between 'unfortunate' and 'complete idiot', and now he was standing in front of her in what was basically a man-dress. And none of this would have really mattered, had she not been so abso-bloody-lutely gorgeous. Okay, not magazine-beautiful, but who's idea of beauty was that anyway? Who needed slim and indifferent, all glacial eyes and perfectly airbrushed skin? The curve and swell of Tamsyn's waist and the fullness of her hips may never meet their standards, but seriously, who cared? Tamsyn was far more lovely than magazine-beautiful.

Tamsyn glanced down at her hands, turning them over and examining them. "Me? Yes, it would certainly appear so." She smiled at his discomfort.

Lopsidedly.

Crap! That made it even worse.

Something about her being present had a soothing effect on Vyvyan. The moment she reached the High Priestess's side earlier, Vyvyan's expression softened. It was like the subtle change in a mother's face when her child enters the room.

Liam snapped his mouth shut. Damn, how long had he been staring? "Hello, sorry, don't mind me, I'm an idiot."

Tamsyn stood up, running her hands over her dress, smoothing the crumpled satin. "Right," she said, moving to stand in front of Liam "Let me have a look at you - see if you're suitable time-travelling material."

Placing her hands on either side of Liam's face, Tamsyn began turning his head to the right and left, examining him intently. Not only did she look lovely, she smelled lovely too. A draught of perfume drifted over him as she leaned in closer; an ethereal scent that seemed to be derived from the same flowers that decorated the room. A light tingling crawled over his scalp as the fragrance floated into his mind, lulling him into an almost hypnotic state. Liam gazed back into her eyes. He could feel her breath across the skin of his cheek. She really was lovely, and she was so close, she was so...

"No," she said suddenly, dropping her hands and stepping back. It was like a bucket of cold water. "Not good enough."

"What?" Kerenza spun round, already moving towards them. "By the Soul! What is it? He is our only..."

"His ears are too big."

Kerenza closed her eyes and turned away from Tamsyn with a shake of her head, clenching and unclenching her hands. "I warned you Vyvyan. I told you, did I not? I told you how she would be."

"Too much drag," continued Tamsyn, "They'll really slow him down. And, who knows? Ears like those could stop the passage of time altogether if we let him loose in the timestream."

"Oh Tamsyn! Do leave him alone." said Vyvyan, smiling.

"Wait, what?" Liam lifted his hands to his ears. Wasn't she supposed to be explaining this whole time-travel thing to him? What the hell was going on?

"I suppose we could tie them back with something. Yes, that might work. It would have to be something truly strong though."

"Pay her no heed Liam, she is like this with everyone. Even me." said Vyvyan.

Kerenza strode back across the room, stopping with her face inches from Tamsyn's. "Yes, well, timeliners are not irreplaceable." Her gaze travelled slowly from Tamsyn's head to her feet and back. "She would do well to remember that we do have others. In case you have both forgotten, this is probably our only chance to recover the Soul."

Tamsyn stepped lightly around Kerenza. "Oh, he doesn't mind, do you Liam?" She touched him on the arm and flashed another lopsided smile.

"Now, now, Kerenza, there is no need to fret. She is only playing with him," said Vyvyan, "I am sure he will be fine."

Tamsyn laughed and spun away in a whirl of fragrance, satin and a glimpse of dimpled flesh. The stray lock of hair broke free of the ivy once again.

Tamsyn paced backwards and forwards in front of Liam. "Okay, now pay attention. There's a lot you need to know, and, as I understand it, you're not nearly as well informed as you should be."

"Yeah," replied Liam, "I suppose you could put it that way."

"Kerenza can be a bit intense, can't she? I expect she simply forgot, she does that sometimes – when it's convenient. Anyway, time-travel is not nearly as bad as you might think. Provided you listen to what I tell you, you'll have nothing to worry about, not a big strapping lad like you." She smiled and winked at him. It was hard not to like her, but really? Jokes at a time like this? "Now, I assume that you already know, as a general rule, time passes much more slowly here than it does in your world."

"Yes, Kerenza did manage to find time in her busy schedule to explain that to me."

"Oh, come now," said Tamsyn, pouting and pulling playfully on Liam's cheek. "Sarcasm? You are better than that, are you not?" This time he did smile back. "But you know nothing of the time-loop, and how we think it could be used to recover the Soul?"

"Not a thing."

"Okay then. Well, the first thing to know is that the time difference between our worlds is not linear. Sometimes time moves faster here, sometimes not so fast. Sometimes it even loops back on itself, connecting our world's present to your world's past. Are you with me so far?"

"Yeah, I think so," said Liam.

"Good. Well such a loop is approaching, and it links to a time in Tiranaral that is just before the Soul was stolen. Anyone using the channel when the loop was active would arrive there in the past. Once in the past, the connection would be just as it was back then, meaning anyone travelling back to Enys Avalen would be in the past here, as well. Still with me?"

"Yeah, but obviously, still looking forward to the part where it's not as bad as I think."

Tamsyn smiled her one-sided smile. "Don't worry, it's coming. Now, once you are back here in the past, it's a simple case of waiting in the Cathedral until the Soul is stolen. Then, follow it back to Tiranaral and report what happened. Understand?"

"Hang on, let me see if I have this right. I use the channel when the loop hits to travel back in time to my world. Then return here, wait in the Cathedral for the thief, follow them, and then tell you where the Soul is."

"Essentially, that's all there is to it," said Tamsyn. "There is one other thing though. Time-loops can cause eddies and rips in local time. It could be nothing more than a little déjà vu, but a big one could... We know a rip will hit Tiranaral just after the Soul goes missing. So, once you're clear of the channel, do not re-enter it. You could be dragged so far back in time we may never find you."

And there it was. Wasn't that kind of his point all along? Messing with time, it was bloody dangerous. "Speaking of getting me back... If I've followed all this right, at the end, all you want me to do, is report back to you what happened to the Soul."

Tamsyn smiled. "Very good. It would appear that you were paying attention."

"Yeah, but I'll still be in the past, won't I? How do I get back to the present?"

"I was just coming to that. Timeliners have a protocol," said Tamsyn. "We're sensitive to anyone out of their native timeline. Time doesn't like it and neither do we. You'll be found, hopefully before any harm can be done."

"Great, so I'm going to be in harm's way as well?"

"Not you! The protocol is there to protect the timeline, you *are* the harm dumbass."

Dumbass? He wasn't a dumbass, was he? And where would she have picked up an expression like that anyway?

Tamsyn was still speaking "Once we have you..."

"Wait, we? You'll be there? But that means…"

"Slow down a bit, will you? Not me, If I'd met you in the past, I would remember it. Whoever finds you will arrange for your return. We'll take care of getting you back to the present. Your main concern in the past," continued Tamsyn, "will be avoiding anyone you know, and not doing anything stupid that could change the future.

"And," said Tamsyn with sudden seriousness, "whatever else you do, it is imperative that you do not return with the Soul. It must remain in the past. If you bring it back the timeline will be altered. So, find out what happens to the Soul - but that's all. We will deal with its return from the present, when the future is still undefined. Oh, and don't look so worried, there is good news as well."

"Really?"

"Oh yes, the fact that you are going into the past rather neatly sidesteps the problem of you spending too much time here. You remember, the part where everything you know and everyone you love turns to dust? Well, since you'll be travelling back in time anyway, you can remain here as long as you like. You'll end up in the past regardless. You're safe to just wait here for the loop, and even better, you get to spend more time with me so, yay, lucky you."

CHAPTER 25

The lavender moon shattered into a hundred fragments before slowly drawing itself back into a wavering whole. Liam sighed and tossed another stone into the river. God, it was a mess.

Vyvyan had been so vulnerable on the bridge that he would've agreed to anything. Then, bantering with Tamsyn, it was all going to be a huge adventure. But this was messing with things that shouldn't be messed with. Screw up here and it'd all unravel into a future where everything he knew was gone - a future where it had never existed at all. The risks were huge. Not pursuing the thief. There was a danger of being caught, sure, but he could keep out of sight, how hard could it be? But time-travel… Jesus, get that wrong and it wouldn't just put him at risk, it would put everything at risk.

And it wasn't just time-travel. Whatever the hell that thing in the Summer Court had been, it knew his name. It wasn't just attacking gateways it was attacking people, and Liam was a target. He'd barely managed to hold it together then. Could he face it again, knowing what he knew now? No freaking way.

If he'd just waited a little while, given himself a chance to think, he would've seen all this coming. But no, true to form, the words had tumbled out without any thought and now he had royally ballsed it up. And how much of that had been to impress Tamsyn? She wasn't going to be very impressed now, was she?

God, it really was a mess.

Gravel crunched beside him. "I was wondering where you might be." Vyvyan lowered herself down next to him on the quayside. "Tamsyn asked me to find you. She has plans for tonight. She thinks you would enjoy an evening out in Lyskerrys as a 'thank you' for agreeing to help us. Although, to be honest, I think she only asked me to come looking for you to get me out of the Cathedral. She worries too much."

When he didn't respond, Vyvyan turned to face him. "Is everything alright Liam? You look worried." She knew his weaknesses as well as he did. He couldn't hide from her.

"Vyvyan, God, I'm sorry. I... I can't do it. It's just too bloody big. I want to, I really do, but I don't think..." He stiffened and almost pulled away when she wrapped her arms around him. This wasn't right, he was a grown man. It was bad enough that she knew how scared he was. But he breathed her perfume, shared her warmth, knew her heartbeat, and melted. It was just the way it had always been, in the days and years before they'd ever met. "I should never have said anything. I'm nothing special. I never have been."

"Do not fret Liam. Let it go, just for a while. You will soon feel better."

"Please don't beguile me Vyvyan. It's really not what I need right now."

"I know," she said. "None of this is your fault. You are trying to undo damage done by another. Whatever happens you will have done your best." She pulled him closer and stroked his hair. "Fear is natural. What we are asking of you is a huge, huge thing. I would be more concerned were you not worried."

"You would?"

"Of course, because it would mean you had not grasped the enormity of it. I know you, Liam. Did you not just entreat me not to beguile you? Why was that? Because beguilement would make it easier to face, and you do not want that, you want to do this unaided. You are more courageous than you think. I would never ask you to do this if I did not think you could. You are too precious to me." Liam followed her gaze out across the river. The spiral arm of the galaxy was scattered across the dark water like blossom. "I would let all this go first if I truly thought you were not capable."

"Really?"

"Really. And if you say no, I still will."

"That's not what I want, but I'm just not sure that I can…"

"You are too hard on yourself Liam. No one feels confident going into the unknown. How could they? They have no idea what to expect. Think back to the time of the Solstice Blade. Your brother, Travis, did he not experience the same doubts? Was he not able to overcome them?"

Of course, all those years ago when they'd set out to find The Solstice Blade. After all the courage he had displayed against the Wild Hunt, Travis had frozen on the doorstep. What was it Celyn had said? Something about there being no courage without fear. She was right. It didn't take courage to face something you weren't frightened of.

"Give yourself a little time. Go with Tamsyn tonight. You will feel differently tomorrow." Vyvyan stood and reached down her hand towards Liam. "Come on, we have a room prepared for you at the Summer Court."

CHAPTER 26

"Really?" said Liam, "A practice run?"

"Well, you looked a bit vague when I explained it all to you, and Vyvyan told me that she spoke to you down by the river, said you were worried." said Tamsyn.

Crap, did she? It looked like there wouldn't be much chance of impressing Tamsyn now, not after that little revelation. "Yeah, actually, I'm a bit embarrassed about that. I suppose I freaked out a bit back then."

"Don't worry, you should've been better informed, it was a lot to deal with all at once. Anyway, I really don't see what you are complaining about. A practice run means you get to spend more time in my company. Sounds like a win-win to me."

"Yes, but we won't actually be going back in time, will we? It'll just be a bit of regular back-and-forthing between worlds. What's the point?"

"Regular back-and-forthing between worlds? Listen to you! You've only done this, what, three times? Also, I'm fairly sure backing-and-forthing isn't even a word."

Liam grinned.

"And," said Tamsyn, "since you ask, the point is to reassure you that time-travel isn't as bad as you seem to imagine, and that you, my Otherworlder friend, are more capable than you think." Tamsyn smiled back and nudged him with her elbow. "We worry about you."

Great, now he felt bad for questioning her - as well as embarrassed.

Tamsyn held up her arm. A copper bracelet glinted on her wrist in the phosphorescent glow from the Summer Court plunge pool. "Okay, this is the Soul. Let us pretend that I placed it under this bench earlier, and now it's gone. So here we are now, the Soul is missing. How do we find out what happened?"

"Easy, we go back in time and watch."

"Good, but we can't just skip back, we have to go through the channel to your world, that's where the time-travel happens, it only works between worlds. So, are you Ready?"

"Er, yeah, but how's this going to work? You aren't a drifter, are you?"

"No, but you can get me through."

"I can? What do I have to do?"

Tamsyn took hold of Liam's hand. "Just this. Oh, and Liam, I am depending on you here, kindly don't let go."

Her hand was unexpectedly soft and warm. Liam's pulse kicked up a gear, it felt like someone had just given his heart a little squeeze. Well, this was interesting, and as for not letting go? Yeah, probably not going to be an issue. He took a deep breath. Whoa, calm down there fella. This was all about the Soul. She wouldn't be interested in him, an Otherworlder, would she?

Liam nodded towards her timeliners' robes. "What if someone sees you in my world?" he said. "You'll look out of place."

"Trust me."

Liam and Tamsyn emerged in the world of men high on Bodmin Moor beside a flooded quarry. Flecks of mica in the granite sparkled in the light of a soft, hazy moon low in the sky.

"That was lucky," said Liam, looking around at the deserted landscape.

"Not really," replied Tamsyn, "I knew it would be remote, and if we are quick, we can ride it back from here too before the gateway moves on. Okay, so if we were time-travelling, we would now be in the past. With me so far?"

"Yep."

"And to get to the past in Lyskerrys we...?"

"We just ride the channel back, I told you, I get all this."

"Okay then - shall we?"

Liam took Tamsyn's hand again, and moments later they arrived back in Enys Avalen at the Ventonana. "Come on," said Tamsyn. "Back to the Summer Court, we only have a little time."

Only a little time? Why did they only have a little time? It was a practice run. They could take as long as they wanted. As much as he wasn't convinced of the need for a run through, it was quite nice that she was concerned enough about him to be worried. He couldn't imagine Kerenza doing that.

Close to the bench where they had started, Tamsyn grabbed Liam's arm and pulled him behind a curtain into an alcove. What on earth was she doing now? Liam peeped out into the night; everything was pretty much as they had left it. Except... except that there was something, there, in the darkness beneath the bench. It looked just like Tamsyn's... but it couldn't be, she never took it off. He turned to look at her. The bracelet was still on her wrist.

"Stop moving!" she hissed, "We'll be seen."

"What? By who? Tamsyn, look, your bracelet, what the hell's going on?"

"And stop talking!"

Liam peered out through the gap in the curtains. What the actual… Over at the bench, reaching underneath to retrieve the bracelet, was a woman, and not just any woman. Open mouthed, he turned to look at Tamsyn beside him. Holy crap… She raised her finger to her lips, winked at him, and nodded towards the gap in the curtain. At the bench the other Tamsyn stood up again, placed the bracelet on her wrist and turned to face him. Liam's heartbeat banged loudly in his head. Shit! She knew he was here! Tamsyn, the other Tamsyn, the one who was not currently hiding with him behind the curtain, smiled her disarming smile, blew a kiss in his direction, and casually walked away, swaying her hips provocatively.

"Okay," said Tamsyn, "so now we know what happened to the Soul. What next?"

"What fucking next? Are you serious? Tamsyn, that was you! We're in the bloody past, aren't we?"

"Well, maybe, just a little bit." Tamsyn squeezed her mouth into a tight line, but her eyes were sparkling. Was she laughing at him?

"Just a little bit? Just a little fucking bit? Can you actually hear yourself? What about all that 'don't encounter yourself in the past' stuff? She, I mean you, past-you, not now-you, saw me. She freaking saw me!"

Tamsyn's shoulders shook until she spluttered, snorting out a laugh. "Oh that. You've no need to worry about that. I am reasonably sure she knows what she's doing. And now you've travelled into the past, and it didn't hurt a bit! And you also know how easy it can be to encounter yourself, I will not be with you next time."

A smile spread across Liam's face. Actually, she had a point, and in a bizarre way it was quite nice that she had found a way to calm him down.

Tamsyn pulled the drape aside. "Come on."

"What? Come on where?"

"We need to know where she's taking the Soul - back to Tiranaral I expect."

"Back to Tiranaral? But she's not… I mean you're not… Crap, you know what I mean! You're not a drifter. How's she going to get there?"

"Oh yes… That bit about me not being a drifter? Not strictly accurate. Amongst my many talents, I am also a drifter."

"So… er… that whole holding hands thing?"

Tamsyn laughed and twirled away from hm. "What? Did you not enjoy that?"

"So, now we know where it went," proclaimed Tamsyn when they returned once again to the Summer Court.

"Yeah, through my bloody letter box."

"Perhaps you can bring it back for me, in the future I mean, I rather like that bracelet."

"And how exactly do we get back to the present?"

"Oh, we didn't go that far back, only a couple of minutes. We can just wait for it to catch up again. Hmmm… I don't know, maybe go for a walk or something?"

CHAPTER 27

Liam leaned against the stone balustrade on the balcony outside his room and looked out over the darkened city. Speaking to Vyvyan at the quayside earlier had made him feel better but not as much as time-travelling with Tamsyn had. Vyvyan had been right about one thing though; he didn't want magical help to deal with this. He had to face this on his own.

Liam inhaled the Otherworld night. The fragrance of gardenias and night lilies curled itself around his worries tangling them up and pulling them away. Smiling, he gazed upwards through half-lidded eyes. The night sky was as alive as an ocean, swarming with nebulae. The floor titled beneath him, and he staggered to one side, blinking the sky back into focus. Bloody hell! He'd succumbed to that pretty quick; it was like being drunk.

A soft, warm, and unexpected arm encircled his waist. Tamsyn pulled herself in close behind him, leaning her head against his shoulder. This was new. The scent of her hair and the perfume she had chosen for the evening mingled with the night. Liam breathed her in, allowing his eyes to drift closed again. His head lolled back against hers.

It was too good to be true.

He fluttered his eyes open. "Wait, are you beguiling me?"

Tamsyn laughed. "Maybe a little bit." Her voice flowed out and became part of the moment. "Why, didn't you enjoy it?"

"It was okay, I suppose," he replied, smiling.

Tamsyn swatted at his shoulder and pulled away from him. The eternal moment moved on and became memory.

"Come on," she said, "I am taking you out to a tavern, I think you'll like it. You'll soon be laughing in the face of time-travel."

Tamsyn hung off Liam's arm chattering and pointing out things of interest, as they strolled through areas of Lyskerrys he hadn't seen before. The streets here were full of people. Some of them were walking and talking, like Liam and Tamsyn. Some of them weren't even people.

On the other side of the street, a group of small creatures trotted past. Their large, bat-like ears flapped around their heads. Tamsyn dug an elbow into Liam's ribs. "Don't stare!"

"God, sorry. It's just…"

She laughed. "I'm joking, silly."

Snatches of conversation and laughter spilled out onto the street as they passed the open fronts of several taverns. It was just like walking past pubs at home. Like the one Jacob's dad worked in. And there it was again. Oh well, that was his bloody loss; let him carry on being an arse if that was what he wanted.

As in most other parts of the town, a tributary of the Ebronndir flowed along the centre of the street. Tamsyn tugged on Liam's arm, and led him to one of the bridges.

Once on the other side, she guided him towards an arched door. His stomach squirmed. It was really happening. He was about to step into a bar full of who-knew-what and experience Otherworld society fully for the first time. Above the door was a sign that read 'The Autumn Sky'.

The sound hit them like a tsunami. People surged past laughing and shouting. Over by the bar a large group broke into song. Liam gripped Tamsyn's arm. She smiled back, mouthing something he couldn't hear and dragged him further in. Her eyes were gleaming. Steering him through the tide of people, she navigated them to a small booth in the corner of the room.

Tamsyn leaned towards him across the table. "There are more sedate taverns," she said, "but this one is the most fun. I swear to you that I saw Vyvyan in here once, although she vehemently denies it."

A waiter in a brilliant satin jacket of green and blue, twirled and sidestepped his way through the crowd towards them. Placing his hands firmly onto the table, he leaned between Liam and Tamsyn. "What can I getcha my friends?" Liam looked up into a pair of wide brown eyes inches from his own. The waiter moved in even closer, tipping his head to one side and peering at Liam through long, thick eyelashes. "Human?"

Liam swallowed and glanced over to Tamsyn. How should he reply? Did people here even like humans? She just smiled, tutted, and rolled her eyes.

"Er… yes," replied Liam.

"First time?" whispered the waiter. His hypnotic eyes filled Liam's vision. He breathed in the scent of warm spice. The man's hair, it was so thick, it was like…

Liam shook his head. "You mean here, at this tavern? Yes. Yes, it is"

"Oooh!" said the barman, stamping his feet up and down rapidly. That mannerism... Liam had seen it before somewhere.

Tamsyn laughed. "I think we'll start with two storm-chasers."

"Then two storm-chasers it shall, be my lady!" replied the waiter bowing low before flicking his head and turning away from the table. He danced away with his short tail wagging excitedly through a neatly tailored opening in the back of his trousers. Liam's mouth fell open. The man's knees bent the wrong way, and where he'd expected to see feet were a pair of perfectly manicured hooves. That was why his odd movements seemed so familiar.

Liam grasped Tamsyn's arm, his eyes were wide with amazement "Wait, that guy," he said, "is he... is he a centaur?"

Tamsyn snorted. "Of course not! That would be ridiculous - centaurs have four legs."

Colour rose in Liam's face. Tamsyn kicked him under the table and winked. "He's a faun." She nodded towards the bar, where their waiter was talking to several other employees. They were trying to look in his direction without making it too obvious. They were failing. "They like you. They don't see many humans."

A short time later the faun pirouetted his way back to the table. High above his head he balanced a silver tray with two elegant, fluted, glasses.

"Two storm-chasers!" he announced, leaning in between Liam and Tamsyn. "Of course, I would never have delivered them by hand if the magic was working properly." Leaving the tray in the centre of the table, the faun danced away again, his hooves clacking loudly on the wooden floor.

Tamsyn pushed a glass over to Liam. "You're going to enjoy this."

Liam eyed the glass nervously. The liquid was a deep chartreuse, but it wasn't the colour that bothered him so much as the movement within. Glassy tendrils of a deeper green coiled through the storm-chaser. It looked almost alive. "Is it okay?" he asked.

"Of course it's okay, silly," said Tamsyn, tipping the glass to her mouth. Liam followed her example and took a swallow. He closed his eyes as the familiar burn of alcohol against the back of his throat reassured and soothed him.

Moments later, he snapped them open again when he heard a slow trickling noise. Tamsyn was very deliberately spitting her mouthful back into the glass in a steady stream. She looked at Liam's half empty glass. Her mouth dropped open and her eyes widened. "You didn't!"

"Didn't what?" replied Liam.

"For the sake of the Soul! Tell me that you didn't just swallow that!"

"What?" exclaimed Liam in alarm. "Of course I did. You just told me to!"

Tamsyn laughed again and took another mouthful. This time she made an exaggerated swallowing motion. "It's fine. Lovely is isn't?"

"I swear one day I'm gonna..."

"Oh, hush now," Tamsyn interrupted, still smiling at him. "You love it really."

Liam shuddered. Was it getting colder? Just a moment ago he had been basking in the soothing combination of strong alcohol on a summer's evening. But now his ears, in particular, felt cold. He placed his glass back on the table and rubbed his hands together to warm them up. Something drifted past his face and he blinked and swatted it away.

"Is something the matter?" asked Tamsyn; a picture of innocence.

"Don't know. Maybe a fly, or something."

A drop of icy water slid down the side of his nose, and again something drifted before his eyes, then another, and another. What the hell? Flakes of snow were falling over his head.

Tamsyn laughed. "That's why they're called stormchasers."

"Magic?" Liam's mouth gaped open. "But... but magic doesn't work anymore."

"It doesn't always work," Tamsyn corrected, "but this isn't real magic; just a little localised weather charm."

"It bloody well looks like magic to me!" laughed Liam. He was grinning like a child now, but he didn't care. This was incredible.

"You try it," said Tamsyn. "The charm's brewed into the drink, so now it's in you. It'll only work very close by, and will wear off really quickly, so you'll have to hurry."

The snow had stopped falling, and the little drifts on his shoulders were beginning to melt. "I don't know how," he said.

"Just think it."

Liam closed his eyes and clenched his fists. A small black cloud formed over his head, and soon a light shower was falling on him. The cloud darkened and rumbled until a spark of lightning spat out and grounded itself on his ear. Tamsyn slapped the table, hooting with laughter. Soon Liam was laughing too, as he blew away the water running down over his mouth. It was going to be a good evening.

Liam's bed swung lazily into view and he lurched across the room towards it before it moved on again. Dropping his wet clothes in a pile on the floor, he flopped down onto his back. The ceiling rotated serenely above him. He was going to regret this in the morning. It had been a bloody good night though, well those bits he could rem'ber... The Soul alone only knew how they'd got back to the Slumber Court...

Stumble Court... the-whatever-the-hell-it-was-called Court. There'd been some staggering about arm in arm, with Tamsyn giggling at everything. An' singin'... an' people of all shapes and sizes poppin' up toastin' them and... Wait, why were his clothes wet again? He rubbed his hand through his hair – that was wet too. Oh yeah, that would've been the detour through the waterfall. Tamsyn's idea, that one. Probably... Hopefully tomorrow wouldn't fill in the rest of the blanks with other things he really shouldn't have done.

CHAPTER 28

Jacob stepped cautiously through the door into the garage. There was already someone waiting inside. How the hell did she get in here? Before he could think anything else, she raised her AK-47 and discharged three rounds straight through his head.

"Fuck!" said Jacob. Honestly, sometimes he wondered why he even bothered. B4z00k4_Ang3l, or whatever the hell her gamer tag was, was clearly a hacker. She didn't even show up on the mini-map for Christ's sake. And a diamond-studded, gold assault rifle - really? The game hadn't even been out long enough to get one of those yet, well, not if you were playing by the rules.

He stabbed at the console's power switch; it wasn't a rage-quit if you had to go anyway. He really didn't want to face Daisy. It was one thing to be told that someone fancied you, but her text message hadn't indicated anything of the sort, and she was bound to have spoken to Liam about the fight. Shit! Why had he lashed out? He'd kept his temper for ages now, then somehow Liam managed to push all his buttons, and before he knew what he was doing, Jacob had punched him. Not hard, it was more of a shove and a fall, but he still felt terrible. It was Liam, for Chrissakes, his best mate - better make that his ex-best mate. He'd better go, Daisy was going to rip strips off him, but it wasn't like he didn't deserve it. She wasn't going to have much interest in him now.

Jacob sighed and closed the door to his flat behind him. You didn't have this kind of trouble with video games. B4z00k4_Ang3l's, intentions had been clear from the moment she placed her first C4 charge and took out most of Jacob's squad. Why couldn't real life be that simple? Since Liam had let slip that Daisy liked him, Jacob had found it hard to think about much else. She was pretty hot; it was amazing he'd never really thought about it before. Well, he'd better get used to the fact that nothing was going to happen now.

Jacob's elbows stuck to the table as he rested his head in his hands and stared out across the pub. It was funny, even at lunchtime, the daylight had the good sense to avoid penetrating too far inside. Respect the gloom. It seemed especially appropriate today.

A pink handbag thumped down in front of him making him jump. "So," said Daisy, "you look like crap."

Shit, she was here. "Thanks, I feel like it. You know - if it makes you feel any better."

"Why would you feeling like crap make me feel better?"

"Wait, aren't you here because of... you know... to give me a hard time?"

"Liam told me you were weird. I thought it was just the computer gaming thing. Was I wrong?"

"Sorry," said Jacob, "Look can we start again? Do you want a drink?"

"That might be a good idea - on both counts. Gin and tonic."

Jacob returned and placed the glasses on the table. Daisy looked at Jacob's glass and then looked up, staring straight into his eyes. "Mineral water? Really?"

"It's the middle of the day, Daisy."

"You're not drinking that shit if you're out with me." Daisy's chair scraped backwards across the floor as she stood up. A few moments later a pint of cider appeared on the table. "There, that's more like it."

Daisy sipped her drink and banged her glass back down onto the table.

"You wanted to see me?" said Jacob.

"Yeah, I was hoping you'd seen Liam, he hasn't been at work all week, and he's not answering my texts or calls. It's not like him. I told work he's sick, but they aren't happy."

Jacob took a long swallow of his cider. Might as well get this over with. "Daisy, look, this is all my fault. He came over the weekend before last, all fired up about some shit or other. We argued, it got a bit physical, and I hit him. It wasn't hard, I swear. God, I really wish I hadn't, I don't know what came over me. I haven't seen him since."

"It can't have been that bad, he's been at work since then, and he didn't say anything to me about a fight. What was it about?"

"I don't really know any more. He was just talking about my Dad and all that… well, you know… and I… I just lost it."

"Your dad? You mean the Lyskerrys stuff? Well, he should've known better than to bring that up."

"What? Why?"

"Come on Jacob, everyone knows that gets to you, even Liam. All the crap the likes of Davy and Beckerleg put you through. It's bound to rile you."

"Yeah, but still, he's a mate. I shouldn't have…"

"No, you shouldn't have, but you did. It's nothing that can't be fixed. Anyway, like I said, he didn't even mention it last week."

Daisy drained her glass and stood up. "Gotta go. Call me if you hear from him, and don't worry."

Well, that was weird, even with his mind befuddled by unaccustomed daytime drinking, Jacob could still tell that it had been strange. Liam had warned him about her personality, apparently you got used to it after a while, but actually, Jacob quite liked it. With all the weirdness going on lately it was nice to have someone taking charge for a change. And what the fuck was Liam playing at? Jacob knew Liam didn't really like his job, but he'd never just not turned up before. That couldn't be because of their fight, could it? Shit, perhaps it was all his fault. Whatever was going on, Liam wouldn't make stuff like that up just to annoy him. Maybe it was time for an apology.

CHAPTER 29

Tamsyn thrust the basket of food and blankets at Liam. "Take these and pass them down to me when I'm in."

Staggering backwards slightly under the unexpected load, Liam struggled not to fumble and immediately drop everything. As he gathered it all into his body, Tamsyn stepped lightly off the quayside and into the rowing boat, causing it to rock and buffet against the quayside. Her footsteps knocked hollowly against the hull.

At some point during the haze of the previous evening, Tamsyn had announced that she was going to take him downriver to a place she called Treth an Wennili. At the time, between his second and third storm-chaser, Liam would have gone along with anything she said. It probably wouldn't have made any difference if he hadn't. It did sound like fun though, a day in the countryside followed by stargazing into the night. And the company? Having Tamsyn to himself again? He could probably endure that.

"Basket," she said, holding her arms out towards him and setting the rowing boat into another cycle of rocking.

Tamsyn absorbed the movement of the boat effortlessly like a living gimbal. Her top half remaining resolutely in position while her hips rocked in time with the hull.

Liam gazed at her. The way she moved... it wasn't beguilement, but it wasn't million miles away either. The swaying back and forth of her hips, back and forth, back and forth.

"Come on, your turn," she called.

Crap! Liam fumbled as he quickly lowered the basket to his waist, almost dropping it. What if she'd noticed?

Tamsyn smiled and reached out to him. He took her hand and stepped down to join her in the boat.

Liam wasn't nearly as confident as she was. Each attempt to accommodate the rolling of the boat was just out of time with it, setting up an alarming oscillation. Tamsyn laughed as he wobbled from side to side. "Sit down," she spluttered, struggling to catch her breath between gales of laughter, "You'll tip us both out!" Liam flushed and sat down with a heavy thump grasping the sides of the boat with both hands. Why on earth hadn't he thought of that for himself?

Although small, the boat was still very ornate compared to the dull vessels of home. Spiralling decoration flowed elegantly along the sides of the hull, but the way the colours spat and stuttered erratically did suggest something wasn't quite right.

The main concession to practicality over design were the rowlocks fixed to the centre of the gunwales and a rough semi-circular notch cut out of the transom at the stern. Both looked like afterthoughts, added recently, and without the elegance employed in the design of the rest of the boat.

Liam nodded towards a number of ornate vessels moored on the other side of the Ebronndir. "Couldn't we have taken one of those?" At the opposite bank several barges bobbed serenely at their moorings. Petals drifted down into the river from the garlands wreathing the barges, and brightly coloured pennants streamed in the light wind.

"Well, we could do. The 'Blush of Dawn' over there actually belongs to the Cathedral…" replied Tamsyn. It sounded like there was a 'but' to come. There was always a "but" when people left things hanging like that.

"But?" said Liam, earning himself a cuff around the ear.

"But," continued Tamsyn, "since the magic stopped working properly there is no way to be sure we'd get back upstream. Before the loss of the Soul, the barges operated magically. All you had to do was ask them nicely, but now we will have to rely on the current to carry us down to Treth An Wennili. Unfortunately, we still have to get back. Look at the size of it. It's far too heavy for us to row. There's a chance the magic might work, but more chance that it won't. It's become so unreliable that we would either be stranded there, or something worse."

"Worse?"

"Further downstream is a waterfall. The current would pull us over. It looks like we are stuck with The Dragonfly. It will be safer to row."

"Wait, what? We're going to row there?" said Liam.

"No, of course we're not going to row."

Liam breathed a sigh of relief. He'd never rowed a boat in his life. He wasn't keen on making his first, probably disastrous, attempts in front of Tamsyn. She'd never let him live it down if he screwed up. It'd be nice to excel at something when she was around for a change, instead of always being, how would Jacob have put it? A noob.

A seat cushion bounced off his head and landed in the bottom of the boat. "Are you okay?" said Tamsyn. "I think I lost you for a second there."

"Sorry, I was miles away. So, if we're not going to row, why did you mention it? I'm pretty sure you said it at least twice just then."

"Because *we* aren't going to row," Tamsyn said flatly. "*You* are."

He really should've seen that one coming.

Tamsyn gazed up at him through her eyelashes. "I couldn't possibly row in these clothes." Liam wasn't convinced. Based on the virtually nothing he knew about boating, flat shoes, wide bottomed canvas trousers, and a smock seemed like perfect rowing attire. But then again… maybe she was giving him an opportunity to do something for her. Yeah, that did seem to make sense. Tamsyn wasn't the type to deliberately set someone up, was she? It was hard to remember her ever doing anything like that. Actually, it was hard to remember much of anything.

She pouted her lips. "Do you not wish to row me?"

Christ yeah, of course he did. And where the hell did she learn to pout like that? They probably don't teach you that stuff in the Cathedral. He couldn't look away from her lips. They were perfect, so full, and soft, and red. Funny how he'd never noticed before…

Liam shook his head. "And you can stop that right now!" he said.

Tamsyn laughed and the beguilement evaporated. Liam turned away, trying to hide his face, but it was too late. Tamsyn had seen him smiling and soon they were both laughing. Surely no one else in Lyskerrys would beguile someone as a joke. He shook his head slowly from side to side. She was something else, using beguilement like that in such a clearly innocent way. "Okay," said Tamsyn, "we'll both row… but you can go first."

CHAPTER 30

Tamsyn rolled over on the blanket and fluttered her eyelashes at Liam. "It's getting dark. Go and get the candles from the boat, would you?" Liam groaned and raised himself from where he sat beside her, rubbing his aching arms. Somehow, he'd ended up rowing all the way to Treth An Wennili. He wandered over to where The Dragonfly was moored at a bend in the river, and soon returned with a basket.

Moving amongst the trees, Liam hung some of the jars from the branches and placed others on the ground. Tamsyn followed, lighting the candles within.

When they had finished, Liam flopped back down on the blanket and looked out over the river. A flock of twilight swallows swooped past the boat. Brief trails of turquoise fire flared in their wake as they carved their perfect arcs and lines through the motionless surface of the Ebronndir.

Gradually, the sky changed hue from the orange of hot forged steel to the impossible velvet indigo of the Otherworld night. On the opposite side of the river, a soft glow appeared through the trees. It took Liam a few moments to realise that this was no evening mist, but the beginning of the Otherworld galaxy-rise.

As the day faded, the slowly spinning galaxy resolved into stunning detail. But the dazzling stars and dust trails of the spiral arm were a mere prelude to the blazing glory of the galaxial core, rising above the trees like a second moon.

"I had forgotten it could be like this," said Tamsyn. "Sometimes you need the presence of someone from elsewhere to remind you of what you have."

She moved in closer. Liam smiled, and breathed in the intoxicating scent of the night, blended with the strange, otherworldly perfume of the fascinating woman next to him. Tamsyn's violet eyes glistened in the light of the galaxy. Was she crying? Maybe not, but it looked like it might not be far off. Liam put his arm around her and pulled her closer. God, he hoped he wasn't reading too much into this. What if she rejected him? What if she laughed at him? He'd always been bad at judging these situations. Tamsyn brushed at her eyes and smiled at him. "Stop it you!" she said, but she didn't pull away.

Suddenly, she turned towards the river, and tilted her head to one side. For just a moment Liam wondered what she was looking for. Then he heard it too. An exquisite trilling echoed across the Ebronndir. Note layered upon note in unfamiliar harmony raising the hairs on the back of his neck.

Tamsyn touched a hand to her chest. "Oh, my Soul! I think it's a swallow," she whispered. "I've never heard one before."

Liam struggled to contain a swell of emotion that threatened to overwhelm him and embarrass him in front of Tamsyn. "Do you believe the legends?" he said.

"I believe they only sing on the last day of their lives," she replied. "I'm sure I would have heard them before otherwise."

"And about it being a bad omen, do you believe that?"

"Silly!" She nudged him sideways with her shoulder, the rare moment of vulnerability now passed. "How could birdsong be a warning of death?" Despite her light tone, she pulled the blanket tighter around her, and pulled her feet in beneath it.

A breeze gusted across the river, flickering the candles and rustling the leaves on the trees. Tamsyn looked back over her shoulder. "Instead of asking awkward questions, perhaps you could make yourself useful and re-light the candles."

Playfully pushing Tamsyn away, Liam raised himself from the ground and made his way to the nearest cluster of trees.

The candles were still alight. He smiled and shook his head. What kind of game was she playing now? He turned back towards the river to call her, but before he could speak something breathed his name.

"Liiiiaaam."

"Tamsyn," he laughed, "what are you..."

Wait, that wasn't her voice.

"Liiiiiiiam. Liam Veeerren"

Little needles of ice began to form in his blood, pricking at the insides of his veins. He spun around. No, no, no! The colour was gone from the flames, and it was draining from everything else too.

He couldn't see clearly. The stars still blazed above him, but of the river, of the boat, and most alarmingly of all, of Tamsyn, he could see nothing. His heart began to pound in arrhythmic terror.

"Tamsyn!"

There was laughter from down by the river. "There's really no need to shout," she said, "I'm right here. Do you need some help?"

"Tamsyn, for God's sake get into the boat. It's the ghost."

"What? Liam? What are you talking about? You shouldn't joke about things like that."

"Now!" he ordered. "I'm not joking. The boat! I'll catch you up, just go!"

"But the fountains... It only goes after the fountains."

"Tamsyn!"

"Oh Liam! For the sake of the Soul! Run. Get back here now!"

Liam launched himself towards her voice, crashing blindly forward through the trees. He was already lost. Whip-thin branches lashed across his face, tracing little burning lines of pain. His foot caught, and he pitched forward onto his hands. Pain burned across his palms, but he was back on his feet in moments. Tamsyn's frenzied shouting was fading. "I can't get past it," he screamed. "Go now! Get in the boat and go."

"Liam, no, I can't leave you!" She was crying, and her voice was shockingly distant.

It was just like in the Summer Court; it was him it wanted. If Tamsyn could just get away. "Go. I can see a way out... Yeah, yeah... light... in the woods. I'll find you, just get out of here."

There was no light. It didn't matter, just as long as she'd believed him. The darkness and noise boiled ever closer. Boulders and tree trunks slammed into him. The sound was all around him now, pressing in on him. Darkness swept around him and over him.

The twilight swallow had been singing for him. He'd never see his home in Liskeard again. He'd never see Tamsyn again. He should have told her he loved her.

He forced his way through branches he couldn't see, ignoring the pain, colliding with tree trunk after tree trunk. His foot snagged, and he tripped. A numbing jolt slammed through his wrists as they hit the ground. Panicked, Liam scrambled to his feet and ran. Stones and rocks span away from his shoes as he fought to stay upright.

His stomach lurched as the ground fell away from beneath him. For a split-second he was falling until hard earth smashed into his side. Then he was rolling and sliding downwards. The fall had knocked the breath out of him, and he sucked in a deep lungful of air, appalled at the thought of breathing the ghost into his body.

Suddenly, his momentum was sapped by a surge of enveloping water. He was in the river. Shit, this was it! He'd never be able to run in the water.

But something else was there, a familiar feeling nudging at his mind. Liam looked inward and there, at his feet, was the gateway. He allowed himself to drop, falling through and into the channel.

***

At the water's edge, there was movement. A small broken body bobbed gently up and down. Its plumage, once vibrant and iridescent, was wetted down and streaked with mud. The last of its colour faded as the ghost enveloped it.

CHAPTER 31

Something hard, solid and low slammed into Tamsyn's shins, stopping her dead. She ran her hands frantically over it: smooth, varnished wood; gunwale; rowlock; tiller. The Dragonfly! She threw herself over the side and collapsed in a tangled heap. Her fingers found wet rope - the anchor line. She grabbed it, wobbled to her feet, and pulled. Pain burned across her palms as it slid through. The anchor was stuck fast. Winding the rope around her wrist, she leaned back using all her weight against it. Finally, it wrenched free and lurched up from the riverbed in a spray of water, sending her tumbling backwards again into the boat.

Tamsyn scrambled to her knees, grabbing the gunwale, and pulling herself up. She was blind, and there was a sound like a great bonfire. She could almost imagine words amidst the cracking, if she let herself. If she wasn't fighting for her life. But they could be words... by the Soul... No! it was saying her name! Tamsyn flew across the bottom of the boat, searching with her fingertips, pushing aside the blankets and flinging cushions over the side. Sudden pain flared across her knuckles as they slammed into a solid pole of wood. An oar!

The boat wobbled and rolled as she thrashed the oar into the water, first one side, then the other. Gradually, The Dragonfly moved out into the river, leaving the ghost behind.

But Liam was still out there. He told her to run. He said he was safe. Soul save him, she hoped he was. This was all her fault. She was the one that brought him here. Fresh tears flowed down over her cheeks. She had no choice; the ghost was closing in, and all she could do was run.

The boat was turning back towards the beach. She had to row from other side. But what little she could see was now blurred by her tears, and her feet tangled in blankets, heavy with river water. She tripped and pitched forward, dashing her temple against the gunwale. Bright patches of light swam before Tamsyn's eyes and the world drifted away.

When the world returned, it was distant, vague, and a little soft around the edges. There was a gentle rhythmic knocking noise. A few feet away the dark mass of the Dragonfly loomed, rocking backwards and forwards. It looked much bigger from down here. Tamsyn was mildly surprised to find she was floating, face up, on the surface of the river. Waterweed brushed over her, feathery and soft. It coiled around her arms and slid over her face. She tried to reach out towards the boat, but her arms wouldn't respond. It didn't seem that important. Something else was important though. What was it now? She had a feeling that she wouldn't like it once she remembered. The water became warm and comfortable., and the long, long tresses of waterweed continued to wrap around her. The world drifted away again.

Stars blazed over her. The water of the Ebronndir lapped at the side of her face, but she couldn't even move her eyes. Soon the river closed in over her as she started to sink below the surface. Why wasn't she floating? People were supposed to float in water, weren't they?

The light from the galaxy flashed through the surface the river as it rotated serenely above. It looked lovely from down here. But as she drifted deeper and deeper it began to fade. What it would feel like when she finally settled on the riverbed? Would it be soft? Would it be like falling asleep? In her mind clouds of sediment settled over her, obscuring the river around her.

In some other life, far from here, someone had once told her that the last of the senses to be lost was hearing. Darkness closed in from the edges of her vision and her eyes gently rolled back in her head. And at the bottom of the deep Ebronndir river Tamsyn fell asleep to the sound of singing.

CHAPTER 32

Liskeard was dark and deserted, a light rain was falling, and footfalls echoed as sharp and shocking as gunfire through the night.

Liam pounded up the steep alley from the Pipe Well and tore out onto Fore Street. His clothes were wet from the river, his hands were bleeding, and terror still surged through him. The ghost was now a world away, but so was Tamsyn. He had to get back to her. God, let her be safe. Please, please, let her be safe.

Reaching the junction with Pike Street, he rounded the corner beneath the clock tower at full speed and raced up the hill. He had no idea where he was going - he hadn't even stopped to think. The moment he was clear of the channel he just started running. His mind was full of her.

But above the clamouring panic, there was one small hope, pushing its way to the surface. He grabbed at it and clung to it like a piece of flotsam in a storm-tossed sea. In the Otherworld he had to be careful of the time; a short time there was a long time here. But, that's the same as saying a long time here is a short time there. He had already been here long enough while Tamsyn was... while she was... but in the Otherworld that was a short time. In the Otherworld it was no time at all.

Time was on his side. From the perspective of Lyskerrys he could get to the gateway almost instantly. It wasn't much, and it certainly didn't mean he could afford to slow down. But it was hope, of a sort.

The gateway! Where the hell was the gateway? In moments he located it - close to the Victorian railway viaduct to the west of the town - bloody miles away. Even with the slower pace of time it might still be too far.

Liam reached the top of Pike Street and staggered to a halt at the fountain. He'd overdone it; run too hard up the hill, and now he was paying the price. His legs shook and his breath burned through his throat. He doubled over, gasping in deep lungfuls of air in preparation for his next sprint.

"You should get more exercise."

Liam's eyes flashed open as a fresh shock of adrenaline jolted through him. "Bloody hell, JJ!" he gasped. "You scared the crap out of me."

Jacob raised himself from where he was lying at the base of the fountain. "Sorry, you did to me too, if it makes you feel any better."

"So, err... you okay?" said Liam.

"Yeah. I... yeah, I think so." Jacob was avoiding Liam's gaze; looking down and twisting one foot from side to side, just like he used to at school.

Liam nudged him in the ribs with his elbow. "I could have taken you, you know, back at your flat," he said with a smile. "Easy."

Jacob looked up. "Yeah mate, I know you could."

He was embarrassed about the fight, but there was something else too - he seemed relaxed, almost serene. No matter, it'd have to wait. Liam had much more pressing concerns. "Look, sorry mate," Liam blustered, his eyes darting from side to side searching for the easiest route past his friend, "but I've really got to go."

"Go? Go where? It's the middle of the bloody night."

"What? Oh, Moorswater, I'll call you. Okay?" Liam stepped left and started to move past Jacob.

Jacob placed a hand on his shoulder. "Whoa! Calm down. Moorswater? What, right now?"

"Yes, really, right now! Look, I'll tell you why later."

"Wait, let me drive you, yeah? It'll be a lot quicker than running. It'll take you about a week anyway judging by the state of you."

Jacob had a point, it would be faster to drive, and his flat was very close. "Yeah… yeah. That'd be great, thanks mate." Now that he had at least a partial plan, Liam felt a little calmer, and began to take more notice of the situation he found himself in. "Sleepwalking again?"

Jacob's brow furrowed. "Yeah… okay, yeah. How'd you know?"

"It wasn't that hard mate. Did you really think you could keep it from me?"

"It's a bit of a relief to be honest. So, what's your excuse for tearing about in the middle of the night?"

"Let's just say I've been having some issues of my own. I didn't want to bother you with them when you were so stressed out, and then… well, we kinda weren't really talking. Look, I don't mean to be rude or anything, but can we get going? It's really important." Liam grabbed Jacob's arm, urging him in the direction of the flat.

"'Course," said Jacob, breaking into a jog back down Pike Street hill. "Coming?"

Liam ran to catch up. "You do know you aren't wearing any trousers, right?"

"Ah, yeah. Unfortunately, not the first time it's happened. Hopefully they're back at the flat."

The door to Jacob's flat was standing open. "Is that something we should be worried about?" asked Liam, holding on to the door frame for support as he caught his breath.

"I'd be more worried if it was shut," replied Jacob. "I got home to find it closed once and had to sleep on the bench under the fountain all night. At least I had my trousers on that time."

Jacob disappeared into the flat, returning a minute later freshly trousered and spinning his car keys around his finger. His *Call of Duty* keyring flashed in the harsh glare of the fluorescent tube in the communal hallway.

As they jogged back down the stairs to his car, Jacob called back over his shoulder. "You still haven't told me why you were out running in the middle of the night."

Damn. He wasn't going to like the answer to that one. "Look, can we just get to the car? I'll tell you on the way. Promise."

Jacob revved the engine hard, shattering the quiet of the night as he raced through Liskeard on the way to Moorswater. In the soft illumination of the dashboard light, Liam chewed on his lower lip. How in the hell was he going to tell Jacob that he was going to Lyskerrys?

Jacob glanced over at Liam. "So, you going to tell me what this all this is all about?"

"You're not going to like it," said Liam.

"Look mate, if it's the Lyskerrys thing again, don't worry about it. I was being a bit of an arse before. When it was all going on at school, you were the only one who didn't act like I was some kind of freak. I should've known you wouldn't try to piss me off. And there was that thing the other night too."

"Well, okay then, yeah, it's the Lyskerrys thing again."

The rain was getting heavier. Jacob flicked the windscreen wipers on and glanced over to Liam again. "Daisy's been worried about you, you know."

"What? You've been talking to Daisy?"

"Maybe. She said you hadn't been at work all week."

"Crap. Yeah, I know, I'll phone them."

"It's okay, she covered for you, but they won't go for it again. So, is that where you were then? The Otherworld?"

Here we go. Jacob might say he was okay, he might even sound okay, but the way his knuckles whitened on the steering wheel told a different story. The rhythmic whirring of the windscreen wipers counted down each awkward second that passed. It was time to face the music.

"Yeah, Enys Avalen, the Otherworld, whatever you want to call it. Your dad was right JJ, it's a real place."

***

"Wait, there's a ghost as well?" said Jacob as he swung the car around yet another bend. In the distance ahead of them the Viaduct loomed, silhouetted against the night sky.

"Yeah, it's basically destroying the place. The fountains mostly - the connections between the worlds - but whatever it attacks starts to break down and decay."

"Alright then." Jacob pursed his lips and let out a long slow breath. "So, if we agree that my dad wasn't making it up, and assume that you aren't actually off your head, why do you need to get back so badly right now, in the middle of the night?"

"Tamsyn, the timeliner I told you about—"

"The hot one, right?"

"Jacob, please - can we focus for a moment? She's in trouble, and I mean serious trouble - could be life and death. The ghost split us up. It trapped me, I had no choice, all I could do was get into the channel and return here. Thing is s-she's... she's still there. It's s-still after her." Liam's voice wavered. Jacob took one hand from the steering wheel, and briefly gripped his friend's shoulder.

"Shit JJ, it was just perfect up until the ghost appeared. The galaxy was rising above the forest, and it's huge, like nothing you've ever seen. We were getting really close, you know? I thought maybe… and there were these birds skimming over the water.

Jacob slammed his foot down hard onto the brake pedal and the car slid to a crunching halt. Liam was thrown forward, his seatbelt biting into his shoulder. "Jesus, what's wrong?" said Liam, turning to face Jacob in alarm. Jacob just stared forward with his hands clamped onto the steering wheel. His lips moved slightly as if he was trying to work something out.

"Jacob!"

Jacob started and blinked a couple of times then slowly turned to look at Liam. "What? Sorry, what?"

"Jacob, what the hell's matter with you? You're freaking me out!"

"Sorry, but what you just said, about the ghost and the woman, Tamsyn. You broke my dream."

"Oh, so just a slight overreaction then, you know, all the braking and skidding and stuff."

"Yes. I mean no. It's weird, but, well, you know how when that happens, when something breaks your dream, how beforehand you have no recollection of the dream at all?"

"Yeah," said Liam, "and?"

"And then, once it's been broken, it's like you tapped into a different part of your mind, and you can't believe you'd forgotten all that?"

"Jacob, I'm sorry, but I'm really in a hurry here."

"I know. I know. Hear me out, it's relevant. Well, that just happened to me only…" Jacob was staring ahead again.

"Jacob!"

"Right, right. Well, when I remembered the dream, it was exactly what you described."

"What? Like déjà vu you mean?"

"Yeah, kind of, but it wasn't that I felt like I'd been here before. I knew it was a dream. But what I dreamed about was exactly, and I mean *exactly*, the same as you described. I didn't see it all though, it was more like a nightmare. I only picked it up when things started going bad. Christ, like there isn't enough weird shit going on at the moment!"

"It could still be some kind of déjà vu though, there might not be anything more to it."

"Alright then, test it. Ask me something I couldn't possibly know, and hurry up, the dream's already fading."

"Alright, I'm actually in a bit of a hurry myself in case you'd forgotten," said Liam. "Okay, okay, I've got something. When I was by the river with Tamsyn, we heard something, can you tell me what it was?"

"Yep," he said, "Birdsong, I heard birdsong, it was bloody amazing actually."

Liam stared. "Bloody hell! I'm not sure how it's going to help though, if you're here and I'm there."

"Too late now anyway, and who says it'll happen again?" added Jacob.

"Yeah, look, I'll think about it, we can talk when I get back, but I really do need to get on."

"Yeah, of course, mate." Jacob put the car back into gear and drove a short distance along the lane until Liam told him to stop.

Pulling the car over to the side of the road, Jacob turned the engine off plunging the night into eerie silence. They both got out of the vehicle, the slamming doors were loud in the darkness.

Liam gripped Jacob's hand in both of his. "Thanks mate, and if you thought that was weird, just wait until you see this." Liam stepped down from the shallow bank into the stream. "Thanks for the lift," he said as he closed his mind and searched for the place within where he knew how to enter the channel.

Water from the stream spun up around him. "Damn," he thought as he slipped into the channel, "why didn't I ask him if Tamsyn made it to the boat?"

CHAPTER 33

Liam skidded to a halt at the door to Tamsyn's rooms. Behind him, starlight flickered through the Summer Court waterfall, and the scent of lilies drifted in on the night air. None of these things mattered.

Please let her be here, God, please let her be here. He hammered on the door until the pain in his hands forced him to stop, but there was no response. Over and over he called her name. Still there was nothing.

A light appeared at the end of the corridor. Liam turned to see Vyvyan descending the stairs from the floor above. Her hair was loose and messy. He'd woken her up.

"Liam? Is everything alright? It's the middle of the night."

"Vyvyan, thank God." He ran the length of the corridor. Patted her shoulders, her arms, smoothed her hair, reassuring himself that she was real. She pulled him to her.

"Liam, whatever is the matter?"

"Tamsyn, is she back? Please, tell me she's back."

"Tamsyn? No, I thought she was still out with you. She said you were going to watch the stars, and not to expect her back until late."

There had been hope. While he was in Tiranaral, when time here was moving slowly, there had been hope. But not now. Now the slow sap of time was crystallising around a timeline without her, a timeline in which she had failed to come home.

The past was set in cold, hard amber, and each passing second dragged their time together inexorably into the past. Those moments by the Ebronndir would be their last. Nothing extraordinary. No time to say goodbye. No telling her that their parrying was covering up something more. He should have told her.

He should have told her.

CHAPTER 34

Tamsyn dreamed she was in a garden. She knew it was a garden because tall, graceful plants grew all around, reaching up towards the light. And she knew it was a dream because the sky looked like water and beams of starlight lanced down through the thick air and danced across her skin.

A woman approached. A woman with large yellow eyes and blue-green hair. A subtle dappling covered her skin. She was, without doubt, the most beautiful creature Tamsyn had ever seen. Cupping Tamsyn's face gently in her hands, the woman moved closer, until her wide yellow eyes were the whole world.

Tamsyn's heart pounded. This wasn't how she would have imagined reacting to this sort of closeness. It felt dangerous and exciting. Was it wrong? It didn't feel wrong. Did it even matter? Because, whatever else it was, it was also a dream, and nothing mattered in a dream. Tamsyn closed her eyes and allowed herself to be pulled in closer. She could worry about it in the morning when she awoke.

The woman with the blue-green hair pressed her lips against Tamsyn's, and breathed air as thick as honey into her lungs.

CHAPTER 35

Tamsyn was surrounded by a liquid gurgling, but it was muffled and indistinct. Mostly the sounds she heard were inside her head. She blinked her eyes open. Waterweed brushed over her shoulder. She was drifting with the current deep in the river. Occasionally she buffeted against the soft mud of the riverbed, raising little clouds of silt that quickly dispersed in the flow. Water blurred her vision, and the thin light that penetrated this far down was a dim and muddy violet. In the distance, mysterious shadows hung in the water. She tried to focus on the trailing weed that flowed over her, but it flicked and pulled away. It was like it knew she was there. How odd; sentient plant life. She smiled at the thought. Somehow the waterweed was moving faster than she was, faster than the current. It certainly was a strange kind of plant, long, thin blue-green fibres with no leaves at all.

And how was she able to breathe down here? Tamsyn tried an experimental breath. There was no rush of choking water, but that was no surprise, it felt like she had been down here a while. In all likelihood her lungs were already filled with river water, and anyway, there was probably no need to breathe once you'd drowned. Was this then what death felt like? Before she could give it any more thought she drifted back into oblivion.

More time may have passed, but Tamsyn had no sense of its passage, nor any way to measure it. A few seconds? A week? Years? She opened her eyes again. She was still underwater, but the river was different here. It was brighter; a soft lilac. Daylight filtered through from the surface, and there was less pressure on her body. Below her the bed of the river continued to flow past no more than a few feet away.

Something touched her cheek. Tamsyn was startled to see a face close to hers, its features made indistinct by the water. A soft, pale hand reached up and touched her eyelids, and instantly she could see clearly. Large golden eyes regarded her with apparent concern. A woman of astonishing beauty hung in the water next to her, parallel to the riverbed. Death, it seemed, was not so bad after all. Tamsyn smiled, and reached out to touch the woman's face, but she darted away as quick as a startled fish. Tamsyn was alone again.

When she next awoke, the woman was back, drifting along in the water next to her once again. "Am I dead?" Tamsyn asked.

The woman smiled. "I do hope not. Your talents are needed in Lyskerrys. The Soul is gone, and there is a ghost at large. I am taking you there now." It sounded like singing.

"I really do think I must be dead," said Tamsyn. "I fell from a boat. I shouldn't be here, deep in the Ebronndir where there's no air to breathe."

"Oh, you did not fall, my love. I pulled you down beneath the water."

"Did you drown me? You look like a morgen. Morgens drown people, do they not?"

"You do not look drowned. Do *you* think you are drowned?"

"Well, it really is hard to say," said Tamsyn. "I certainly don't seem to be breathing, and you *did* pull me in to the river."

"I pulled you in to save you. I gave you the Morgen's Kiss," said the morgen.

"That was you? I thought I had dreamed it. But in that case, I must be drowned. The Morgen's Kiss is just another way of saying that someone has drowned."

"No, no, no, my love. The Morgen's Kiss is the kiss of life. Your kind cannot breathe underwater, so we share our breath with you."

"Well, I am very grateful to you then, and since you are not drowning me, is there anything you would ask of me in return for your kindness?" asked Tamsyn.

"I will ask nothing of you now," said the morgen, "but your kind generally do not think well of ours. There may come a time when one of us needs help. That will be my price."

Tamsyn considered the morgen's request. It didn't seem unreasonable considering that she was not going to drown her, and she was going to take her back to Lyskerrys. And anyway, since this was either a dream, or she was already dead, what harm could it do to agree?

"You morgens are not so bad," she said.

"Yes," agreed the morgen, "we are not so bad."

CHAPTER 36

Many things were a mystery to The-man-who-didn't-know-who-he-was, but he knew that there were spirits in the forest. He would hear their whispers as he descended into sleep. He would catch their movements from the corner of his eye as he crossed the walkways strung between the tree trunks. He would feel the air move as they passed him in the deserted libraries.

The man was not afraid of the figures that drifted between the trees, because The-loveliest-woman-in-the-world told him that they weren't real ghosts. She said that they were memories - memories that didn't realise their time had passed and their cities were lost. She also told him that the magic in the forest was really only a memory of magic too, and that was why it couldn't be relied on.

Even though The-loveliest-woman-in-the-world told him these things, the man found it a little hard to believe. He may not know very much, but he knew that memories didn't usually stay around in the world. Not like that, not as something almost physical, at least his didn't. The-loveliest-woman-in-the-world would never deliberately deceive him, so perhaps she had simply got it wrong. And so, The-man-who-didn't-know-who-he-was decided that the best thing to do would be to ask one of them. That way he would know for sure if they were spirits or if they were just memories.

The very next morning The-man-who-didn't-know-who-he-was climbed to the top of one of the high watchtowers that stood above even the tallest trees in the city. And there he found a spirit.

The spirit ran from one side of the wide platform to the other, leaning over the balustrade and calling down. When she moved, she flowed like water, and when she shouted there was only the softest whisper, but the man could hear what she was saying.

"Who is Kern?" he asked, "and why are you calling for him?" But the ghost did not hear him, or if she did, she chose to ignore him. And so, the man decided to ask her a different question. The man knew that spirits did not tend to stay around too long, and so he decided it would be a good idea to get straight to the point. "Are you a spirit?" he asked. "Or are you just a memory who doesn't realise that your time has passed, and your city is lost?"

The spirit turned to face The-man-who-didn't-know-who-he-was, and he could see that she was crying. He wondered if she was crying because she had heard his question and did not like the suggestion that she might be a memory. The man felt sorry for the spirit then, but the spirit ran through him as if he wasn't even there and whispered the name again with all her might out across the whole of the forest for no one ever to hear but the The-man-who-didn't-know-who-he-was.

In the end the man decided that the spirits probably were just memories after all, and that it was probably better that way.

CHAPTER 37

"We were separated," said Liam. "Out at Treth an Wennili. The ghost… it appeared just as the sun went down and separated us. I told her to get to the boat and get away. But everything was fading so fast I don't know if she made it. And then the ghost drove me into the river. By pure luck, I found a gateway back to my world, and I came back here again as soon as I could. I thought… I hoped she would be here."

Vyvyan brushed her fingers against her lips, chewing at her nails. She was trying to hold it together, but her hand was trembling, and her eyes were wide in the darkness. God, the bond between Vyvyan and Tamsyn - the bond he'd shared in the Summer Court - if anything happened to Tamsyn it would destroy Vyvyan.

Vyvyan's fingers fluttered over Liam's arms, and she glanced from side to side. Her eyes never settling for more than a moment before moving on. Words tumbled from her mouth, one on top of one another. "She could be okay… if she got to the boat, she could still be okay. Could she not?

She would have listened to you. Yes, yes, of course, she would... We have to get back to Treth an Wennili. She could still be there, if she escaped, she could still be there."

A commotion shattered the silence outside Vyvyan's room. Someone was shouting; sharp and urgent in the quiet of the night. They ran to balcony. Something... there! Over at the riverbank, a short way downstream from the bridge. People were running from their homes and gathering at the quayside. There were raised voices, but they were too far away to hear what was being said. One or two jumped down onto a small beach at a bend in the river. A fresh swell of panic built within Liam and he turned and ran out into the corridor. There was someone in the water. God, what if it was Tamsyn?

As he closed in on the crowd, a sickening sense of inevitability settled in Liam's stomach. There was something on the beach. It looked like a body. People were crouched on either side. No, not her. Please don't let it be Tamsyn.

A light flicked on down by the water. There was a glint of bright copper. It had to be a timeliner, no one else wore armlets like that. And timeliners were rare - really rare Kerenza said.

Liam leapt from the quayside, but he'd jumped too soon - he wasn't going to make the beach. Glowing water exploded around him as he smacked down into the shallows. The shock of the impact jolted through him, jarring his back. Despite the pain, he kept running. Ploughing through the river, he kicked up plumes of spray as the water dragged at his legs threatening to trip him. He stumbled and lurched on to the beach, struggling to remain upright.

The crumpled figure was obscured by the gathered crowd. But there were glimpses as people milled around the body. Dark hair trailing onto the beach - too dark to be hers, but it was wet, streaked with sand and, wreathed in waterweed - that would make it darker. And it curled the way

Tamsyn's did. A flash of clothing; cropped canvas trousers. It was her.

"Tamsyn!" The voice was his, but it sounded like someone else – someone very far away. He barged his way through, unable to slow down as he tried to stay on his feet. Reaching the still, prone, form of Tamsyn, he threw himself down on the beach next to her. He took her head in his hands. No, no, no, please no! Only shock dammed the tears.

Her face was cold, but... but not that cold. Shouldn't it be colder? It would be colder if... if she was... but no, there was a trace of warmth! And there, the slightest twitch of her mouth. Her chest – there was movement, shallow, but definitely there. Then her eyes flickered. She was alive.

Tamsyn coughed. Once, twice, and then rolled to the side, retching. Liam tried to help her up, but she pushed his arms away from her, like someone waking from a deep sleep.

"It was a morgen." The woman's voice drifted over from somewhere in the crowd. "I saw it lift her out of the water, lay her here. Dived back in the water as soon as it saw me, it did. Dived back into the river and was gone."

"Morgens drown people," said another fearfully. "Why would a morgen save her?"

"Do not be so daft," replied the woman, "morgens do not drown folk, that's just old tales and nonsense."

Tamsyn sat up on the beach, her hands sinking into the soft, wet sand on either side of her as she struggled to support herself. Looking around dazed, her gaze settled on Liam. "Liam? What...? What in the world am I doing here?"

Sitting between Vyvyan and Liam on the quayside, Tamsyn leant against the older woman for support. Once it had become clear to the gathered onlookers that Tamsyn was unharmed after her encounter with the morgen, they started to drift away, and the night had been allowed to seep back in. In fact, Tamsyn was recovering remarkably quickly for someone who, only minutes ago, had been found unconscious on the riverbank.

"Wait!" she said, grasping Vyvyan's hand. Her back stiffened. "We can't stay here. The Cathedral – we have to return to the Cathedral!"

"The Cathedral can wait," replied Vyvyan rubbing Tamsyn's hand. "The first thing we need to do is ensure that you are unharmed."

Tamsyn felt the tell-tale presence of an empath in her mind as Vyvyan's consciousness connected with hers.

"Vyvyan!" she said, mentally pushing the other woman from her, and physically moving away to support herself. "I appreciate your concern, I really do, but there's no need to examine me. I assure you I'm fine."

Vyvyan clucked and ran her hands over Tamsyn's arms. "You were just brought back from who-knows-where by a morgen, I need to make sure that you were not harmed."

Tamsyn grasped Vyvyan's arm, forcing her to look. "How long was I out? Vyvyan! How long? The time-loop… we only get one chance at this. We have to be ready. We must get to the Cathedral. There will be time for recovery later."

CHAPTER 38

"Think of it as a wave," said Tamsyn. "You can see the swell coming for quite some time, but when it starts to build, things will happen very quickly. The connection to the past is only made when the wave breaks. It's like a tube, a complete circle, but it won't last for long."

Liam was back underground in the Cathedral with Tamsyn, Vyvyan, and Kerenza. It wasn't a room he had ever been in before. According to Vyvyan, it was used for training purposes and contained various tools and aids to help newly discovered timeliners develop their skills.

In the centre of the room was a low circular platform encircled by a shallow moat. There was something around it - some kind of railing. Liam tried to focus on it, but the moment he did, his ears started to buzz, and a flat ache spread rapidly out from his temples. He screwed his eyes closed and turned his head away. "What the hell's that?"

"Time barrier," said Tamsyn. "It helps keep the student grounded in their own time. Try not to look at it. It'll give you a headache."

Liam rubbed his temples. "Right, thanks for the warning. I mean it's a little late, but thanks. And all this equipment - you use it to sense the loop?"

"Only since we lost the Soul. Everything is harder now. I would've been able to do this unaided before, but these days I need the familiarity of the training tools. Even so, I'm not sure it will be enough."

Tamsyn crossed a small footbridge over the moat and stepped onto the platform.

"Do you have the gateway?" enquired Vyvyan.

"Yes, it's still here," said Liam. "It doesn't feel like it's about to move either."

"And the Soul?" said Kerenza. "You are sure you know what you are looking for?"

Yes, he knew what he was looking for. That wasn't really the problem at the moment though, was it? Kerenza, as usual, seemed more concerned about the plan than anything else. "Yes, Kerenza, an aquamarine jewel the size of an apple."

There was movement up on the dais. Tamsyn had picked something up from the floor, a sphere made of the same headache-inducing material as the railing. Liam took a step closer. "Okay?" he asked looking back at Vyvyan.

"Yes, you will be fine." Vyvyan moved to stand behind him and placed her hands on his shoulders. Liam relaxed a little. At least someone seemed to be concerned about how he felt about all this. All that talk about facing up to your fears was all well and good, but standing here, right now, preparing to violate the laws of time, well, that was some scary shit.

Up on the dais, Tamsyn moved her lips, repeating a phrase over and over. Whatever she was saying, Liam couldn't make it out.

Her performance was impressive though. No matter what anyone might think of her personality, it was hard not to be reassured by the quiet professionalism she was displaying as a timeliner. Liam rolled his shoulders and rocked his head from side to side, releasing the built-up tension in his muscles. This was what she'd trained for. He was in good hands.

Stiff fabric rustled right beside him, making him jump. Kerenza! Bloody hell, she was like something out of a horror movie sometimes. "Put this on," she said. "It will help you in the past." She pushed something cold and hard into his hand, then stepped back, wiping her hand against her robes.

You. She'd said it will help *you*. Not it will help the Soul. Was he reading too much into this? "What is it?"

"An evanescence charm. It will help to keep you… out of sight."

"Like invisibility?"

"Not really, it discourages people from seeing you. A bit like a mixture of camouflage and amnesia, but not really either. It will make you even more insignificant and forgettable than usual. Quite useful really, if you do not want to attract any attention."

Liam turned the pendant over in his hand. It looked singularly unremarkable; a dull, tarnished copper colour, like an old coin. There were markings, possibly symbols, on it, but they were too heavily worn to read.

"Doesn't look like much," he said.

Kerenza stiffened, her jaw muscles tightening. Damn, that wasn't how he meant it. "And these days, it. Is. Not." She spat out each word like a bad taste. "Like most magic since the loss of the Soul, it is unreliable at best. I am sure you are correct. It won't help you in the slightest." With that, she folder her arms and turned her back to him.

"It does not work here, now," Vyvyan said, giving his shoulders another squeeze, "but in the past, provided you make it back to before the Soul was lost, it will afford you valuable protection. You may not need it, but do not forget that no one in Lyskerrys will know who you are. Back before the Soul was lost, we had never met. You may not want to draw attention to yourself."

"Wait, what? Provided I make it back? You mean I may not end up in the past?" This was just great! Something else Kerenza had conveniently forgotten to mention.

"No, no, do not worry. You will be in the past. But it is not completely accurate, especially with the unreliable nature of magic these days. There is a chance that when you get there, the Soul will have already been taken."

"So how will I know?"

"If you are back before the loss of the Soul, check the charm. You will know," Vyvyan said.

A splash in the moat diverted Liam's attention. A shoal of small fish circled the dais, glinting in the Cathedral's subdued lighting. One flicked itself out of the water in a flash of silver, before splashing back down.

"Termynnow," said Vyvyan, following Liam's gaze.

"Sorry, what?"

"The fish, they are called termynnow. They are sensitive to time disturbances and are attracted to the time-loop and by what Tamsyn is doing." Another fish splashed heavily back into the water. Tamsyn scowled. Were they distracting her? Christ, he hoped not. He was relying on her to keep him safe when he caught the time wave. Another termynnow jumped out of the water. Liam winced and glanced up to Tamsyn, awaiting her reaction, but the expected splash did not happen. At the apex of its arc the fish simply popped out of existence. "Whoa! What the hell was that?"

Kerenza spun to face him. Her eyes were wide. Shit, she was scared. How bad must it be to worry Kerenza? All his submerged fears boiled to the surface again. "What?" she snapped. "What did you see?"

"That fish, it jumped out of the water, and then it just disappeared!"

"It is okay Kerenza," said Vyvyan. "The loop must be close." Turning to Liam she said, "Do not fret, they like to play in the time stream, it will return again soon."

As she finished speaking, a small splash announced the return of the little fish to local time.

Liam glanced over to Tamsyn. She was deep in concentration with her back to them. In front of her, a light mist was beginning to form in the air.

"She is manifesting the loop," Vyvyan explained. "Ordinarily they pass without anyone noticing, except for timeliners who are naturally sensitive. The loop does not really affect us, it is the temporal relationship between our world and others that is changed. But Tamsyn is manifesting it, so that it will be apparent to you. That could cause you some disorientation and confusion. Be on your guard."

Well, that's just great; disorientation and confusion as well? Like he hadn't already experienced enough of that! "Okay, so is there anything I should look out for?"

"Yes, many things, but the most important is to try and keep track of our current timeline."

"Keep track of the current timeline? What does that even mean?"

"Because the loop will be visible, you will start to experience time distortions that you would not ordinarily be aware of. You really just need to pay attention and try and ignore anything that you know is not from the current timeline."

"Time distortions? So like things slowing down and speeding up?"

"Yes, or things merging between timelines."

"Okay, slowing down, speeding up and things merging," Liam said.

"And anything that is just plain weird," added Vyvyan.

Was that a joke? She wasn't smiling. Liam's stomach twisted. "Weird? Wait, weird in what way?"

Tamsyn called down from the dais. "Here it comes!"

Shit, shit, shit!! It was happening too fast. What the hell was he was supposed to be doing again? Didn't he have some sort of coping strategy for when it all kicked off? His mind spun. Just push through it, think about it later.

Up on the platform Tamsyn was moving her arms about like someone trying to balance on a moving object. Her eyes were tightly closed, and her brow was drawn down. Christ, even her teeth were clamped together. He hoped she knew what she was doing, because it looked like she was struggling, dividing her attention between several things at once. Suddenly, her arms started to blur. Each balancing movement trailed ghostly images of itself.

"Remember the wave Liam! This is the water drawing back from the shore as it builds," called Vyvyan.

Each of her words stretched out and overlapped the one following it creating a strange echoing effect. Liam tried to reply, but after the first word the delaying effect confused him so much that he was unable to continue.

"Try not to speak!" said Vyvyan. "Focus on the current timeline. Do not allow yourself to become distracted."

Tamsyn called out again. "We're in the tube!"

In front of her, the mist had coalesced. The school room around them was dissolving into the air; elongating, distorting, and being dragged into the haze. Vyvyan's caution not to speak was regurgitated back at them as a bizarre reverse echo.

Suddenly the mist reared up and over Tamsyn's head, dropping down onto the occupants of the room. Liam was in the centre of a tornado of repeating words. Some of them were his own, and some of those he was sure he hadn't even said yet.

The haze exploded outwards, and the room filled with past and future versions of four of them. The more bizarre of the possible futures were easy to identify, but not so easy to ignore.

In what had to be the current version of the moat, termynnow were leaping out of the water in frenzied shoals. Disappearing at the top of the wave and then reappearing back where they started. In one of the many other versions, they all lay belly upward and motionless on the surface of the water. He tried not to focus on that reality.

"Liam, don't go!" screamed Tamsyn, "It's too dangerous." No, that wasn't from this timeline, those words came from the one with the dead termynnow. All around, were visions from Liskeard: people going about their everyday lives. Some of them were blurring like Tamsyn had done, stretching away into the past and the future. One of them was Liam himself, when he caught up with Kerenza at the Pipe Well.

"Liam! Now!" shouted Tamsyn.

In one timeline, maybe even the one he was supposed to be paying attention to, Kerenza flowed towards him like a figure from a long exposure photograph. She placed her hands on his shoulders and shook him.

"Liam, the channel now!" she said.

"Now?" Liam replied, three or four times before he actually said the words.

Liam watched as he stepped out of his body, trailing multiple copies of himself behind him, and walked towards the water. It was the one with the dead fish. He watched himself stop and look around unsure of what to do.

But in this timeline, he knew exactly what to do. It was time to go. Though a blurring of motion created by his myriad other selves he stepped forward, into the gateway.

CHAPTER 39

The reflection in the mirror was very satisfying. The man allowed himself a smile. The only familiar feature was the wrinkling at the corners of his eyes, his own mother wouldn't recognise him. A long black scarf was wound around his head leaving only his eyes visible through a narrow horizontal slit. One end of the scarf trailed down his neck. He turned his head to one side to admire the effect it created. In another time he could have been an Arabian assassin.

The only illumination in the small room was provided by a table lamp, and the way it lit him from beneath was pleasingly dramatic.

Dressed entirely in black, he would be difficult to see in the dark, or at least he would be in this world. Where he was going, things would be rather different. It was never truly dark there, not in the way it could be here. Long after the sun had set every detail would still be pin sharp. The light might be gone, but the detail would remain in a thousand velvet shades of night.

No, his real advantage would be the element of surprise. No one would be expecting something as audacious as this. In fact, no one would be expecting anything at all, it would never even occur to them.

Yes, surprise was going to be his friend on this mission, that and his secret weapon.

With the transformation complete, the man turned away from the mirror and opened the door. It was time. Stepping into the darkened hallway he stopped as the door clicked closed behind him, his hand still holding onto the handle.

There was just one more thing he needed. He was surprised he had forgotten it.

CHAPTER 40

With a sound like heavy furniture being dragged through another room, thunder ground across the Cornish sky. Liam glanced up at the dark clouds as he climbed the stone steps from the Pipe Well and laughed - why would a little rain concern him? He was in the past, and it was like a dream.

Years of science fiction films and novels had educated him in the art of cautious time-travel: change nothing that could corrupt or abandon the native timeline, and never, ever, encounter your past self.

He knew the risks, but... the past! He was in the fricking past! Okay, so it was only a few weeks in the past: before he had caught up with Kerenza at the well, before he had ever met Tamsyn, and before he had any recollection that there was such a place as Lyskerrys. But, hell, it was still the past!

Everything was waiting for the rain. The buildings stood out brilliantly against the black sky, as the last of the sun's rays lanced in below the clouds, and the wind had dropped to nothing. The world was holding its breath in anticipation of the storm. Liam pulled up the hood of his sweatshirt and turned onto the steep alleyway that led up to Fore Street.

Excitement threatened to overwhelm him, but he had to remember why he was here. He had to get back to Lyskerrys in the past, and to do that he needed to locate a gateway. A quick mental search revealed that it was currently in a tributary of the East Looe river at Moorswater.

The weather was unusually stormy, and that had only happened once recently that he could remember - the morning he met up with Daisy at the café. It might not be the same day, but it was similar enough to make him nervous. Liam took out his phone and checked the date.

"Holy crap!" he said, quickly looking around to make sure no one had heard him. It was two weeks before his first visit to Lyskerrys. It had to be the same day. It would be too risky to take the direct route. He'd have to divert past the train station.

Liam turned left out of the alleyway, heading away from Pike Street and any potential meeting with Daisy. He gazed around in amazement. Everything he saw, everything, had already happened. He'd lived this day before, and even though he couldn't change anything, he knew what was going to happen, and that knowledge was intoxicating. For all of his life, for all of everyone's lives, the past was gone. And yet here it was. Again.

It was hard not to stare at the two-week-old versions of everyone he passed. The first one or two were absolutely terrifying – what if someone spoke to him? Would that be enough to send him along a different timeline?

He made it about halfway to the junction with Bay Tree Hill without incident. So far, so good. Perhaps he was worrying unnecessarily. Even on days when he wasn't actively trying to avoid contact, he didn't often stop and talk to anyone in town. Slightly more relaxed, he allowed his gaze to shift into the middle distance - and caught someone's eye. Crap! It was Davy, loitering at the other end of the road.

Instantly, Liam dropped to one knee, pretending to tie his shoelaces. Perhaps Davy hadn't noticed. Some chance, Davy had seen him alright; there was no mistaking that nasty little smirk on his face.

A small knot of people crossed from one side of the street to the other, blocking Davy's view. It had to be now. Liam turned and hurried back along the road towards Pike Street. It was far from ideal, given that this was the day he'd met up with Daisy on the hill, but Davy was bound to try and cause trouble. At least he knew what Liam-in-the-past was going to do, and anyway, he might not even be there yet. If he was quick, he could avoid Davy and get to the top of the hill before he and Daisy even showed up.

Dipping his head, Liam put as much distance as he could between himself and Davy. At the junction with Pike Street, he edged around the corner and scanned the hill. There was no sign of Daisy. With a relieved exhalation he hurried up the hill.

He made it almost half-way to the top before things started to go wrong.

"Liam!" called an insistent voice from somewhere down the hill behind him.

He Froze.

"Hey, Liam! What's the matter? You ignoring me?"

Shit, oh shit! He had been recognised - it was Daisy. Think! What was he going to do now? He quickly turned to face a shop window, maybe she'd think he hadn't heard her, at least he'd pulled up the hood of his sweatshirt as he left the Pipe Well.

"Liam, wait up!" she called again.

Shit, shit, shit! What had Tamsyn said? Something about not doing anything stupid and screwing up the future - how's that working out?

Daisy's hand clamped down onto his shoulder.

He was caught.

"Sorry," she said, wobbling on one foot and using Liam to steady herself, "bloody heels."

Daisy reached down and adjusted her shoe. "Liam!" she shouted. Liam jumped. She called out again. "Hang on!" To his utter amazement, Daisy carried on up the hill. She had somehow failed to recognise him.

But if she was on her way up the hill, that could only mean one thing... Liam glanced out from under his hoodie after her.

For a fraction of a second, he couldn't place the familiar figure waving at Daisy. Then the world began to press in around him. He knew that face; it was the face he saw every morning in the mirror, he just wasn't used to seeing it on someone else.

Liam slumped against the shop window. God, he felt awful. His head was thumping, his limbs were shaky and weak, and he was suddenly very hot. Sweat broke out on his forehead, and he pulled the constricting neck of his hoodie away. He had to cool down. And if he didn't sit down soon, he was going to fall. It wasn't just the shock of seeing his past-self further up the hill. Something else was wrong. Time did not want this encounter to happen.

"Alright Daise?" Liam heard himself say, "Sorry, I was miles away. How's things?"

Was that really what he sounded like – all weird and tinny?

"Yeah, not bad thanks," she replied. "Look, shall we go to Java Joe's? We're going to get soaked any minute, we can get a coffee and something to eat, I'm starved."

The first isolated raindrops began to patter against Liam's hood. With his eyes beginning to roll in his head, he risked another sideways glance up the hill. They were heading his way. Thunder boomed overhead rattling the shop windows, and rain began to pour from the sky.

"Are you okay?" he heard Daisy say, "'Cos you look like crap. Come on, you'll feel better once you've eaten."

"What?" replied past-Liam. "Oh, sorry. Yeah. Java Joe's. Great idea."

Daisy hooked her arm through his and began to guide him down the hill in Liam's direction.

Crap! Java Joe's was the bottom of the hill. Daisy was pulling past-Liam closer to the wall, but they were still headed straight for him! God, what could he do? There had to be some way to distract them. They hadn't encountered each other the last time this happened, when it was him walking down the hill with Daisy. Something must have been different, what the hell was it? His phone! Of course, the phantom phone call! Fighting nausea and confusion he jammed his hand into his pocket. His world was going dark around the edges but he was able to pull it free and scroll through the contacts. Come on, come on, come on! Where the hell is it? His field of vision constricted to almost nothing. Until all he could see was a single line of text – Daisy (Work)

As he started to slide down the glass to the pavement, Liam stabbed his finger at the screen.

Somewhere far away, a phone began to ring.

"It's you, you're butt-dialing me." It sounded like Daisy was at the end of a tunnel.

"No, I'm not. It's off, look."

In the shop doorway, Liam's surroundings began to swim back into focus; his vision was returning. He looked up the hill. His past-self was sitting down on the kerb, and Daisy was showing him her phone.

Now, he had to move now! Turning away from them, he staggered down the hill. He could turn into Fore Street and lose them as they went to the café. But now that the effects of encountering himself on a past timeline were wearing off, he began to recall how this bizarre situation was going to play out.

To be more precise, he knew how the situation had played out last time it happened. The time when Daisy didn't have a chance to answer her phone.

Shit! Liam fumbled and nearly dropped the phone as he stabbed at the screen again. He had to cut off the call.

As he ducked around the corner into Fore Street, he could just hear Daisy's voice. "It's rung off, must've been a glitch, come on, let's get out of this rain before my mascara starts to run."

Rain hissed against the granite flagstones of Fore Street as Liam looked out from under the Guildhall arches. On the other side of the road, Daisy and his past-self walked by, arm in arm and dripping wet, chatting contentedly. In the fifteen minutes he'd been in the past, Liam had covered barely any distance and only avoided disaster by the narrowest of margins.

At a little footbridge over the East Looe River, in the shadow of the Moorswater viaduct, raindrops were popping off the surface of the water like little wet fireworks. Liam was soaked through, but it didn't matter. The gateway to the channel was here, in the stream behind a row of cottages close to the railway line.

With a final quick glance around to ensure he was alone, Liam lifted his leg over the railing and dropped down into the water.

CHAPTER 41

Liam arrived back in Lyskerrys at the remote fountain where he had first seen the decay - or should that be the fountain where he would see it? If his experiences in Liskeard in the past had taught him anything at all it was that he'd have to be a lot more careful in future.

Past.

Whatever.

He smiled at the new ways he could find to say the wrong thing now that time-travel was a factor.

The first thing he needed to do was to confirm that he'd returned to a point in time before the Soul was stolen. According to Kerenza, if this was the case, the magic would still be working, and so would the evanescence charm. Liam unzipped his hoodie to check it where it hung on a chain around his neck.

"Holy crap!" he gasped, stumbling backwards. If he hadn't collided with the fountain behind him, he would have fallen over.

A shaft of brilliant aquamarine light lanced out through the opening in his hoodie. Liam fumbled frantically to block it with his hands whilst still trying to retain his balance. Jagged shadows jumped out from the buildings and statues opposite, swinging about wildly as the light found new exits between his fingers.

A few moments later, his hoodie was zipped up again and the light concealed. Liam leaned back against the fountain panting and looking around to check that he hadn't been noticed. How the hell this thing was supposed to stop him being seen was a mystery. Still, at least he seemed to have returned to the right time; the charm had never lit up like that before.

Before returning to the Cathedral, Liam wanted to see how Lyskerrys was faring in this time. And so, instead of heading back towards the town, he walked around to the back of the fountain to where Vyvyan had pulled away the piece of stone.

Last time was here, the stone slid away easily from the fountain like lifting a scab from a recently healed wound. Liam ran his fingers slowly across the smooth surface, there was no indication of any of corruption at all. He had arrived in Lyskerrys' past, and for the moment the Soul was safe.

All he had to do now was get to the Cathedral and wait for the thief.

CHAPTER 42

Far below the Ventonana fountain, Liam's footsteps slowed as he passed under the archway into the chamber. Then, he stopped moving altogether, and simply stood, eyes wide and mouth open.

The Soul of Lyskerrys was here.

Vyvyan, Tamsyn, and Kerenza had all spoken to him of the Soul. They had tried to tell him why it was so important to them, about the love that the Soul had for every one of them. He had even lived through the awful loss Vyvyan felt when the Soul was stolen. But those words and those emotions, came nowhere close to preparing Liam for being in the Soul's presence.

He was overwhelmed.

The Soul was love and warmth and joy. It was like standing beneath the stars and knowing that your tiny spark of life was part of the everything, both insignificant and essential at the same time. How could words convey this when they were only sounds? The Soul was beyond sound, beyond light, beyond even emotion. But he belonged to it, belonged to it more than he had ever belonged to anything. And it belonged to him, they were a part of the same thing.

Christ, this was what they had lost. No wonder Vyvyan felt the way she did, no wonder Kerenza would do anything.

Liam laughed. Something tickled his cheek. He raised his hand to his face. What was that? He turned his hand in the air in front of him, entranced by the glistening of his tears in the light of the Soul. He laughed again and looked around. There were people here, people everywhere, and he was supposed to be keeping a low profile. He tried to stop. It was like trying to stop the sunrise.

The sound of running water, chatter, and birdsong filled the air, and there, beneath a white marble cupola in the middle of the chamber, was the Soul of Lyskerrys. Aquamarine light sparked through curtains of water that flowed inexplicably upwards around it, collecting in inverted channels in the roof.

There was no way anyone could take the Soul without being seen, not with all this activity. It was too easy – all he had to do was wait. He must have looked a right twat in front of Vyvyan earlier, worrying that he couldn't do this. There was going to be nothing to it. Selecting a chaise longue close to the chamber wall with a clear view of the Soul, Liam settled down to await the thief.

Half an hour passed. There were still a lot of people around, and none of them looked like they were planning on going home any time soon. Liam swung his feet up onto the chaise longue and lay back. Well, there was no harm in making himself comfortable. A long sigh escaped his lips as he settled into the soft cushions and folded his arms behind his head. He'd definitely notice if anyone tried to take it.

Liam opened his eyes and stretched. A slow smile spread across his face. He felt bloody fantastic. Wait… he hadn't been asleep, had he? Nah, he'd only closed his eyes for a second. Propping himself up on one elbow, he yawned and rubbed his free hand through his hair. Okay, maybe a bit more than a second, but definitely no more than a couple of minutes. Although... Liam stretched and looked around the chamber. Where the hell had everyone gone?

Liam rubbed his eyes. That was weird, he was sure it had been brighter than this a moment ago, when he'd first opened his eyes. It was pretty quiet, too, a lot quieter in fact, now he stopped to think about it. Obviously, with no one here the murmur of voices was gone, but there was something else... God, why was it so hard to think? The water - that was it, he was sure that he could still hear it when he first stood up.

Over at the cupola, the peculiar backwards waterfall was no longer flowing. The water in the channel was adhering to the standard laws of gravity. Maybe that was just something that happened when the chamber was empty too. Did magic have to be conserved? Did you save magic in the same way the you saved water and electricity? He was getting distracted again. He stood up and tried to focus.

The bright ring of metal on stone, followed by a long drawn out rattling echoed across the chamber. It seemed familiar somehow, but it was so hard to think. What on earth was it? It wasn't something he would have expected to hear in the Otherworld.

Wait, a coin! That was it. It was the sound of a coin hitting the floor. Liam snapped back into full alertness. In all the time he had spent in Lyskerrys he had never once seen anyone using money. However people here paid for things, he was pretty sure they didn't use cash. And anyway, he was alone in the chamber. There was no on here to drop a coin, even if they had one.

In moments Liam was across the chamber. It may have looked like a coin; the dull gleam of tarnished copper against the stone floor, but he knew immediately what it was. He patted at his chest. The evanescence charm was still beneath his hoodie, securely attached to its chain. But…? But if he still had his charm then where the hell had this one come from?

All the pieces dropped into place. The light had dimmed because the Soul was gone. That was also why the reverse waterfall had stopped. And the reason he had such difficulty noticing any of this was there on the floor in front of him. Someone had used an evanescence charm to cover themselves while they took the Soul. Clearly, they hadn't intended to drop it, because Liam's thoughts were now much clearer, and his mind was racing. He glanced over to the cupola; it was empty. How long had it been since he heard the charm rolling across the floor? Three or four seconds? More? There was no time to waste.

Sprinting across the chamber, Liam tore out into the room beyond. The sound of retreating footsteps echoed down from high up on the staircase. He wasn't far behind. He pulled the evanescence charm out from beneath his hoodie and gave it a quick kiss. "Time to do your job," he whispered and then raced up the staircase, pursuing the thief of the Soul of Lyskerrys.

***

Liam staggered to a halt at the bank of the Ebronndir, wheezing. Jesus Christ, he really had to do something about his fitness levels. The sky was dark, and the streets were deserted, and in the centre of the river a boat was manoeuvring. It had to be the thief.

Great, now Liam needed a boat. On the other side of the river, subtle pulses of light flowing along the silver scrollwork marked the location of The Blush of Dawn, the barge he had seen on his day out with Tamsyn. He'd lose time crossing the bridge, but he had no choice. He'd almost lost the Soul once by falling asleep. He wasn't going to let anything else get in his way. He sprinted up and over the bridge and clambered aboard.

How the in the hell were you supposed to drive these things? There was nothing that resembled a wheel or tiller anywhere in sight. But there was magic – that was apparently still a thing in this time. What had Tamsyn said when they had taken the Dragonfly out for the day - something about asking it nicely?

"Follow that boat!" he said, "…please." Even with no one around, he still felt foolish, but to his amazement the Blush of Dawn began to gently glide forward and out into the Ebronndir.

***

A dull roar filled the air, and clouds of spray rolled and billowed above the river. The Blush of Dawn drew into the bank just short of the waterfall. Liam hopped from foot to foot. The thief was already clambering out of his own boat, Liam was going to lose him. Before the barge had finished pulling into the riverbank he was over the side and splashing through the shallows.

The thief disappeared into a stand of tall reeds – Jesus, that guy was fast. Liam sprinted in after him, his lungs burning, he could taste the salty tang of blood, and he was getting so bloody hot. He had to get his hoodie off, but if he stopped and lost sight of the thief, he might never find him again. Liam crashed out of the reeds and into a clearing. The roar of the falls was suddenly loud in his ears. The thief was out on the stones, heading towards the midpoint of the river. Still running, Liam whipped the hoodie up and over his head and swung it under his arm. Something arced away ahead of him, glowing a rapidly fading aquamarine through the night.

"Shit!" It was the evanescence charm.

A moment later Liam realised the mistake he'd just made. Out on the lip of the waterfall, the thief stopped and looked back. For an instant their eyes met. Liam had been seen.

The charm's glow winked out as it landed in a sod of grass a few meters ahead. Liam threw himself forwards grabbing at the dewy grass as he hit the ground. His fingers closed around metal, and somehow his momentum rolled him back onto his feet again, and he staggered back into a run. The evanescence charm was, miraculously, safe in his grasp.

Out on the rocks at the black edge of the world, the thief stopped and squinted back over his shoulder. Then, as if nothing had happened, turned away and continued his comically exaggerated stepping from one rocky protrusion to another.

At the midpoint of the river the thief stopped and stared upwards at the stars, just as Liam edged out onto the first of the rocks. Whatever the thief had planned, Liam had to follow him. He had to know where he was taking the Soul.

Liam stepped onto the third stone, and the thief stepped off the edge of the world.

CHAPTER 43

Jesus Christ, he fell fast – instantly beyond any hope. The thief dropped away, rolling and twisting. Any sound he made was swamped by the deafening roar of the water. There was no way back.

Unable to breath, unable to tear his gaze away, Liam was already painting a crimson picture in his mind of what was going to happen when the man hit the rocks. He didn't want to see this.

Time slowed; a cruel courtesy allowing Liam to absorb every dreadful detail. The thief was picked out in obscene contrast like a fly on a wedding cake. A small, black figure amongst the colossal plumes of glowing, churning, dirty-yellow foam. For a moment he vanished into the maelstrom, but then he was back, flung around like a lifeless doll. The rocks raced up to meet him. And then, the instant before he hit, searing shafts of light blazed through the water.

The thief was gone.

Liam gasped in a lungful of air. The channel! He must have entered the channel. In the excitement of the pursuit

Liam had never once thought to check where the gateway would be. But he could see it now, gleaming and fizzing a few feet above the rocks at the bottom of the waterfall.

Liam followed the path of the plunging water with his eyes. He was going to have to jump.

There was no way he would have the courage if he stopped to think. But his legs felt like they weren't his own. On either side, the water of the Ebronndir roared and plunged past, billowing spray into the air, and distracting Liam as he tried to calm himself. He'd probably already left it too long, by the time he'd fallen to the gateway it could be gone, and he'd explode against the rocks. It was going to close, and the Soul would be lost forever.

He focussed on moving his legs. Reluctantly they began to obey. His mind retreated, appalled by his actions. Do it for Tamsyn! Do it for her! Liam gritted his teeth and forced his shaking legs to move. And then, horrifyingly, he was over the edge.

God, did he really just do that? The falling water kept pace with him even as his mind shut down. He opened his mouth to scream, but no sound came. He wouldn't have heard it anyway over the crashing of the water on the rocks below. The rocks that were screaming towards him. But somehow, he was calm. There was nothing he could do now. It was out of his control.

And then he plunged into the channel.

Liam crashed forward into a chaos of light and noise. At the base of the Pipe Well stairs, the Soul blazed like an earth-bound star. Light seared across the visible spectrum with an intensity that was almost audible, shaking the very air. Beyond, the thief was on the floor, eyes wide with terror, kicking out with his legs and trying to back away through a solid wall.

The Soul was growing, changing. A piercing shriek permeated the enclosure. Shapes were beginning to form, coalescing within the dazzling light. Gradually, an unmistakably human form started to emerge. The soul-light continued to dim and then, suddenly, it blinked out. What remained looked like an elderly woman. But her features hadn't settled. It was impossible to make anything out. It was as if the Soul was still trying to understand what it was in this reality. Her face flowed and rearranged itself.

Wailing incomprehensibly, she radiated fear. Her arms were pulled in protectively against her face, and her shoulders were hunched. It was like she was trying to shrink within herself. She jerked from side to side, looking around in terror. Then she began to tremble. She was frightened of everything, like each new sight was more horrible than the last.

Her gaze settled on the thief, and she began to move towards him, reaching a thin, trembling arm out to him. The thief's eyes grew even wider, and he scrambled frantically at the wall behind him, desperate to get away. But her legs wobbled, and she sagged sideways into the wall. Liam caught a glimpse of her face. It seemed be settling, the disconcerting fluidity was easing. Something about the form the Soul was adopting seemed oddly familiar. Before he could think any more, she was moving again. Liam launched himself to the side as she staggered back across the chamber.

Something moved. In the trough near the iron gates that closed off the well there was a glint of silver. What the hell was that? It was gone before he could look. But he'd seen it somewhere before. God, he couldn't think with all the screaming. It happened again. Another. And another. Flash, flash, flash. Termynnow! A whole shoal leaping into the air from the trough and then disappearing. The water seethed and boiled with them. No! The time-steam. Tamsyn had warned him; the loop would cause eddies and rip tides that would ripple out across the local timeline.

Liam slammed into a wall, as the old woman barged past him, easily catching him off balance and forcing him aside. He turned his head to follow her, and for a fraction of a second their eyes met. She was terrified. Tears were streaming down her face. She was lost. She was in a reality she didn't belong in. A reality that she didn't understand, and that didn't understand her. But it was too late. She was running towards the trough, the fish, the channel. And then she was gone.

Liam stood open-mouthed staring after the Soul. It had all happened too fast. There was nothing he could have done to prevent it. The Soul was lost. She had re-entered the channel. She could be anywhere in time. But he'd seen her face, and not for the first time either. He knew who she was.

Liam sagged against the wall and exhaled. At least he knew what happened to the Soul. Based on that criteria the mission could be judged a success. The fact that she had transformed, and then got lost in time was unexpected, but that was a problem for Vyvyan, Kerenza, and Tamsyn. He'd been told not to interfere in the past, and he hadn't. It was a reconnaissance operation and he had reconnoitred – assuming that was a thing. What he needed to do now was find the gateway, return to Lyskerrys, and wait for a timeliner to get him back to the present.

In the sudden quiet of the well, the light from the evanescence charm began to fade. He hadn't even noticed it was glowing until then. From somewhere down near the floor, a soft whimpering drifted up. The Thief. Liam had to get away from here before the effect of the charm wore off and the man noticed him. That would be a disaster. If the thief caught sight of him, he would know immediately who Liam was. The old woman was not the only person at the Pipe Well that night that Liam recognised. If he didn't get out before he was seen, the timeline would be corrupted beyond repair.

CHAPTER 44

Sunlight sparkled off the lilac water as Liam walked along beside the Ebronndir. It was a lovely day. In fact, given that he was still in the past, it had been a lovely day at least once before. Tamsyn's instructions had sounded simple enough, especially after all the subterfuge and time-traveling and what have you. All he had to do was return to Lyskerrys with information about the fate of the Soul, and sooner or later a timeliner would find him. What he hadn't been expecting was to feel so exposed and uncomfortable while he was waiting for them to turn up. Not that he had been there very long, and not that he was actually doing anything wrong, his discomfort was more centred around the potential for disaster.

Trying to decide on the safest course of action was proving to be tiring. Was it safer to be on the lookout for potential problematic encounters or did that just make him look shifty and suspicious?

Perhaps the safest thing was to do nothing; the less he did, the fewer mistakes he was likely to make. Yeah, he just needed to find a quiet spot to wait it out. If his presence in the past was that much of a red flag to the timeliners, they should have no trouble finding him, no matter where he was. Following the Ebronndir, he eventually reached the quayside above the little beach that the Morgan had bought Tamsyn all those days ago.

Would bring Tamsyn to.

In the future.

Christ, even thinking was tiring in the past.

Lowering himself to the ground in what he hoped was a natural and unsuspicious way, Liam sat down on the quay wall and idly swung his legs backward and forward over the side. It was oddly comforting. The sun was warm on his face and soon he was feeling much calmer. Jumping down to the beach Liam sat down on the sand, leaned back against the quay wall, and closed his eyes. If anyone did happen to see him down here, they would hopefully assume he was sleeping and leave him alone.

"Don't. Say. Anything. Just get up and follow where I lead."

Liam froze, but his was mind racing. He must have dozed off. His arms were chilled and dotted with goosebumps. He glanced upward - the sun was now obscured by clouds. An uncomfortable dampness soaked through the seat of his jeans from where he had been sitting on the sand. But more surprising than any of that was that he knew the voice. It was Tamsyn.

But it couldn't be. She said it wasn't her that found him in the past, that she would remember if she had. But hers wasn't a voice he was likely to forget. What was he supposed to do?

"Tamsyn! Thank God it's you. I thought..."

"Be quiet! For the sake of the Soul just stop talking," she hissed. "I have no idea how you know my name, and I have no desire to know. No good will come of using it. Now do as I say and follow me."

"But..." began Liam.

"Just do it," she said. "The longer you're out here, the more danger you're putting us and yourself in. Get off your backside and follow me."

CHAPTER 45

The most recent addition to the list of things that were unknown to The-man-who-didn't-know-who-he-was was his current location. That is to say that he knew roughly where he was in relation to the forest city, having travelled here with The-loveliest-woman-in-the-world, but the place and its purpose, were a mystery. What he did know was that he would much rather have remained in the place that had been all he had ever known.

Leaving the city in the trees had been a difficult thing for him to do. But The-loveliest-woman-in-the-world had told him they needed to go, and he trusted her. He had always trusted her, and he could see no reason why that would not continue to be the case.

At the same time as she told him they had to leave she had also informed him the time was close when his memory would be returned to him. The-man-who-didn't-know-who-he-was was not so sure about that either. He may not remember much, but what he did remember was blissful. His life in the forest city had been happy, and whilst it was true that he may have only known one person, that person had been The-loveliest-woman-in-the-world. In addition, until recently at least, his world had been full of magic. The-man-who-didn't-know-who-he-was had a feeling it would be hard to improve upon that. He may not know many things, but he knew that regaining his memory was unlikely to make him any happier than he had always been.

The-loveliest-woman-in-the-world had also told him that until the time was right for him to remember he would have to remain hidden. Although she didn't say why, he assumed that was the reason he was in this place now. Looking around, his best guess was that he was currently in some kind of cave. It was quiet and there was no natural light, but it was not completely dark. Candlelight lapped at the walls, breathing life into the shadows. The man was not worried though, The-loveliest-woman-in-the-world had assured him he was in no danger and he had absolutely nothing to be afraid of, and that was good enough for him. His trust in her was complete. All he had to do was wait in the cave for her to come for him.

When The-loveliest-woman-in-the-world returned, the man was surprised to see she had brought someone with her. Approaching the man, she took his hands gently in hers. "This lady is a soul breather," she said, "you don't know her now, and you don't know what it means to be a soul breather, but you will very soon." The woman wore a long aquamarine robe, and the way she carried herself suggested that she held a position of some authority amongst soul breathers, whatever they might be. The-man-who-didn't-know-who-he-was was largely unconcerned, all he really needed to know was that The-loveliest-woman-in-the-world was with him.

"It's time for your memory to be restored," The-loveliest-woman-in-the-world said. "You may find the process a little traumatic and disorientating, but this lady will be able to smooth the transition for you.

"The questions you've wondered about for so long are soon to be answered, but I want you to remember that there was a man in the forest city with none of those answers, he was a good man, and he was loved."

The-man-who-didn't-know-who-he-was might not know much, but he knew one thing, and that was that he didn't like the way this sounded. It seemed as though The-loveliest-woman-in-the-world was saying goodbye, but the way she squeezed his hands and looked into to his eyes made him feel that everything would be okay. But, just to be sure, he tried to commit the way she looked right now to memory.

He memorised the way her violet eyes sparkled in the candlelight.

He memorised the way her tumbling chestnut hair came loose from the band of twisted ivy that fought so hard to contain it.

And he memorised the way that the light flowed around the copper armlets that adorned her arms.

He memorised all these things as the blocks in his mind drifted away like thistledown.

Liam knew who the soul breather was. He had always known who she was, well, at least since he had first dreamed of her. But he did not acknowledge her. Not yet. All he could do for the moment was gaze into Tamsyn's eyes.

It was a strange feeling. He knew Tamsyn the way he had known her before his memory was closed off to him, but he also knew her the way he had known her in the forest city. She was the only person he could ever remember knowing, and the only person he ever needed or wanted to know, as The-loveliest-woman-in-the-world. The feelings that he had before the forest city, which, now he had returned to his own time, was technically only moments ago, didn't quite match up to the way he felt about her now. He held tightly to her hands. He briefly wondered if he should be embarrassed about how things between the two of them had been in the forest, about how he had adored her there. The feeling soon passed. He wasn't embarrassed in the slightest.

CHAPTER 46

"How is your memory now?" said Kerenza. Liam looked up at her from where he sat holding Tamsyn's hand. Kerenza was agitated, pacing back and forth across the floor of the Cathedral, with her arms folded tightly across her chest. She must have asked the same question three times already. Liam, got it, of course he did. He'd experienced the Soul for himself now, but still, give him a bloody chance. His memory might be back but fitting the events together in order was proving to a problem. From their point of view, he'd only just left for the past. But he still had what felt like months' worth of forest memories to slot in around it.

"Give him time Kerenza," said Tamsyn, "you know as well as anyone that it can take a while to adjust after a memory occlusion." Kerenza bridled and turned to glare at Tamsyn.

It was starting to come back though, but it was still bloody hard. Whichever set of memories he focussed on, forest city or his life before, the other took on the quality of a dream, like it never happened. It was making his head hurt.

"I think I can do it," he said, "let's give it a go." Kerenza was at his side in moments, her green eyes wide in anticipation. He'd have to— what was the expression again? — manage her expectations a little. "Just take it easy though Kerenza, will you? It's all still a bit mixed up in my mind."

Kerenza moved in close, until her eyes were inches from his. "Well, you had better spit it out now then, before you have another of your episodes."

"Kerenza!" snapped Tamsyn.

"Oh, please!" Kerenza rolled her eyes. "Do not suddenly try and act like a responsible adult, Tamsyn. Do you really think your behaviour would be tolerated were not it not for your... favoured status in the Cathedral? We do not have the time for this constant pandering to his human need for special treatment."

Jesus! What was her problem? "For Chrissakes Kerenza! This is already hard enough for me. Do you want me to tell you what I remember or not? I thought this was important to you!"

Kerenza tapped her foot and then, very slowly, turned to face Liam. She narrowed her eyes. "Continue."

"Thank you. Okay, travelling to the past was fine. I ran into a bit of trouble in Tiranaral through, someone saw me, someone I knew, and in avoiding him I ran into myself."

"What!" Tamsyn's grip tightened on his hand. "You saw your past-self?" She'd gone pale.

"No, no, it's okay, he didn't see me. I mean I didn't see me, crap, look, you know what I mean, right? There was no contact." Tamsyn loosened her grip again and stroked his arm with her free hand. His memories were getting slippery again, and the room... had it changed in some way from before he left? Liam surveyed the chamber. The cupola was still there, the alcoves, the water channels, all still present. It didn't feel the way it had when the Soul was here, but nothing looked obviously wrong. Kerenza was tutting and shaking her head.

Tamsyn scowled up at her. "Liam?" she prompted.

"Yeah? Oh, sorry. I got back here before the Soul was taken. The charm worked like… well, like a charm I suppose. No one saw me."

No, hang on a minute… something still wasn't quite right. Crap, why couldn't he think clearly? He glanced around the room again. Nothing. It was so bloody frustrating.

"Can we *please* get on with it?" Kerenza was pacing again, and as she turned back towards him, the stiff fabric of her turquoise robes rustled across the flagstones.

Liam shook his head. "Right, yes. Sorry. Anyway, when I was in the Cathedral, here, it all became very vague. I couldn't seem to keep my mind focussed on anything. Anyway, I heard this sound…"

Wait, Kerenza was wearing turquoise. That wasn't right. Turquoise was the High Priestess's colour. Kerenza wasn't High Priestess, she was a soul breather—Vyvyan! How could he not have seen that? "Where's Vyvyan? She should hear this."

"She is not here." Tamsyn said twisting her hand free from Liam's.

Okaaay, what the hell was that all about? Apparently, he'd hit a raw nerve. And pulling her hand away? She'd never acted like that before. Something he said must have seriously pissed her off, but it was still so hard to think. Perhaps it hadn't come out right.

"Yeah, I can see that," he said, "but she's the High Priestess, she's closer to the Soul than anyone. She should be here."

Kerenza paced back to Liam's side. "Things here are more fluid than you are accustomed to. I would not expect you to understand," she said. "I am High Priestess now.

Anything you have to say can safely be told to me. You may continue. Tell us what happened to the Soul."

Kerenza was high priestess? But he'd only left for the past minutes ago. Liam shifted in his seat to look at Tamsyn. She was staring down at her hands. "Well, er... the thief, it turned out that... that he..." He glanced at Tamsyn. She turned her head away. Was she avoiding eye contact? How could everything change so much, in the space of moments?

"Liam," snapped Kerenza, "Try and focus. Is that something a human can manage?"

"A... a charm, he had an evanescence charm."

He really couldn't take any more of this, he had to know what had happened. "Tamsyn, what's wrong? What just happened? Where's Vyvyan?"

Kerenza cut in. "Vyvyan is no concern of yours." She stopped in front of Tamsyn, turning her back towards him, like he wasn't even there. There had to be a sensible explanation for what was going on. He was getting nowhere trying to figure this out himself. He'd ask Tamsyn straight, at least he'd know what he was dealing with, and it would show Kerenza he didn't give a toss what she thought.

"Look, Tamsyn, I feel like I've done something wrong, or said something to upset you, only I literally have no clue what it is. Why won't you tell me where Vyvyan is?"

Suddenly, Tamsyn was on her feet, she took a step backwards away from the couch, pushing past Kerenza to face him. Her face was pale, and her eyes were wide. "Liam," she snapped, "you've got to stop talking about Vyvyan. She won't be coming back. She's dead."

CHAPTER 47

Christ! He was on the wrong timeline! Something had gone wrong in the past. Liam surged to his feet, stumbling towards Tamsyn, reaching for her. He hadn't done anything, hadn't changed anything. He'd been so careful. Sweat broke out on his forehead and his breathing grew fast and shallow; useless adrenaline, preparing him for a conflict he couldn't win. No wonder Tamsyn had almost freaked when she thought he'd met himself - she must have sensed something was wrong. He snapped his head around, scanning the room. Everything looked the same, but how could you tell? It could be anything... differences in the carvings on the wall, or the way Kerenza's hair fell, or the absence of someone who should be here, someone like Vyvyan.

Liam grasped Tamsyn's hands, his heartbeat banging in his head. "Something must've gone wrong in the past," he spluttered.

"What?" said Tamsyn, "Liam, you are scaring me... nothing went wrong. Why would you think anything went wrong?"

Nothing went wrong? Could she even hear herself? "Because of Vyvyan!" he shouted at her. He shouldn't have shouted, but he was in the wrong time – nothing mattered now.

Tamsyn was twisting her hands in his and trying to pull free. "Liam, I just do not understand. What do you mean 'Because of Vyvyan?'" She was looking at Kerenza, begging for help with her eyes,

"Of course you bloody don't," Liam snapped, "because for you nothing's changed. When I left, she was alive, and now, in this timeline, she's gone, and you are all used to it. For Chrissakes Tamsyn, if it wasn't for you two… if you hadn't sent me into the past, she'd still be here."

Tamsyn stopped pulling against him. Her eyes narrowed, and she stared straight at him.

"Tamsyn, no, wait…"

She pulled a hand free and slowly peeled his fingers from the other.

No! How could this have happened? He'd avoided himself in the past. Okay, Daisy had touched him, but she didn't know who it was. There was nothing else, unless… shit! Of course, Davy. Davy had seen him. He'd probably followed him and seen the whole thing.

The floor tilted and Liam staggered sideways. The room spun drunkenly around him.

"Liam."

Who *was* that? She sounded a hundred miles away.

"Liam? Is everything alright?"

Alright? Of course he wasn't al-bloody-right.

Another voice. "Liam!"

Tamsyn? A Tamsyn. Some freakish other-time Tamsyn, not his Tamsyn. The chamber spun; a blur of motion, making him fairground-ride-sick. His peripheral vision darkened, and then everything: light, sound smell, touch, slammed into him, forcing him back and back and back until there was nothing left but darkness.

Was someone calling his name? It could be, but it was a long way away. Or underwater. Or something...

"Liam."

There it was again. Jesus, his head hurt.

"Mmmm... What?"

"Drink this." Cool metal pressed against his lips. Liquid flowed into his mouth. He spluttered. *Swallow, you're supposed to swallow – idiot.* He forced his eyes open. The roof of the Chamber of the Soul arched away into darkness, but most of his field of vision was occupied by the faces of Tamsyn and Kerenza.

Kerenza spoke first. "Liam, I need you concentrate now. Tell me what happened to the Soul."

Tamsyn glared at her.

"This is important Tamsyn, or have you forgotten? We cannot risk him having another episode like that. What if the next one is worse? What if he forgets everything he found out?"

"For the Soul's sake Kerenza, I won't allow you treat him this way." Tamsyn placed a hand on Liam's cheek and moved close, until her violet eyes were everything. God she was lovely. "You had a panic attack. Kerenza beguiled you to send you to sleep."

Yeah, that was right... something had happened, hadn't it? Something he should be concerned about, but then again, maybe not. If it was that important it'd be right at the front of his mind, wouldn't it?

"She has lifted most of it," said Tamsyn, "the glamour, but not completely, not until we understand what's wrong." Oh, perhaps something was wrong. Tamsyn wouldn't say it if it wasn't true. No, she must be mistaken. He'd ask Vyvyan, she'd know, sometimes it seemed like Vyvyan knew everything.

Shit.

Vyvyan.

There it was.

Liam was upright in a flash, flinging his legs off the chaise longue, pushing himself to his feet. Kerenza was on him in an instant, gripping his shoulders and gazing at him. He slumped back, thoughts receding. Tamsyn eased him back onto the chaise longue and sat down beside him, placing her hand on his arm. "Liam, you don't need to worry. You're not on the wrong timeline."

"I'm not?" Tamsyn sounded pretty sure, and if anyone would know it'd be her. But there had been something, hadn't there? "Are... are you sure?"

"I'm a timeliner. I know. I would sense it if you were in the wrong time. It's how I found you in the past in the first place. You're safe. Breathe deeply."

"But... but... what about Vyvyan? You said she was... dead."

Tamsyn's eyes flicked up to Kerenza's.

Kerenza shook her head.

"Lift it," said Tamsyn.

Kerenza exhaled. "Fine." Turning to Liam, she let her gaze linger on him.

Tamsyn drew a slow breath. "And she is." She closed her eyes and turned slightly away. "She... died while you were away."

"But she was here when I left. I wasn't gone that long. Not long enough for..."

"She had been ill for a long time," said Kerenza, her expression softening for a moment. "You would not have known."

Was it the dark place he'd seen when he shared her mind? Was that what it was? "Okay, okay. Let's say that I'm not on the wrong timeline. Let's say Vyvyan really is dead."

Wait, did Tamsyn just wince? "For Christ's sake Tamsyn, Vyvyan's dead, don't you think you should show a little remorse?"

"Liam, please… I don't understand why you're getting so angry." Her voice trembled. But it was too late now. He shouldn't pursue this, he was going to hurt her, but there were a few things she needed to hear.

Kerenza looked over to him. "Liam, don't…"

"Don't what, Kerenza?" It wouldn't hurt *her* to hear a few home truths either. All she'd ever done was manipulate and belittle him, and now what? Just shut up and do what you are told? "Don't tell her that it's not okay to act like Vyvyan didn't matter? Don't tell her that just because I'm not one of you that my opinion doesn't count? Well it does, Kerenza. Vyvyan deserves better than this, and she deserves better than you."

Tamsyn said nothing, but tears flowed down her face. She really didn't understand. Okay, so there were differences between the Enys Avalen and his world, but so what? He hated the way Vyvyan was being forgotten, but as Tamsyn ran from the chamber, Liam hated himself too.

***

"Liam! You must not say her name!" For the sake of the Soul! Would he never grasp this? Kerenza crossed to the entrance of the chamber, parted the curtain and stole a glance through. Empty. That was something at least. If anyone heard him… She shuddered even thinking about it. There were limits, even for a High Priestess.

"But Vyvyan is gone. How can you be okay with that?"

"Keep your voice down! It is not okay to grieve here." And humans wondered why they were always made to forget. "This is not your world. You must not name the dead and you must not grieve." Oh, look at his little heart break. She had to remember they were like children. Things had to be simplified for them. And she was High Priestess now. Was it not her job to educate? "Liam, believe it or not, I know you are in pain. I do not understand this need you have to express your loss, but it is a huge taboo here. The biggest."

"It's like no one cares that she's gone."

Kerenza sat on a chaise longue and patted the seat next to her. She was not entirely heartless. "We care. You do not understand. It is not the end— not like it is for you. She is with the Soul, but she was an empath, and if you show grief, she will feel it in the next life as surely as she would have in this."

Liam sat heavily next to her. He looked defeated. "You wanted to know what you did to upset Tamsyn? You insist on speaking of the dead Liam, and Tamsyn does not understand the ways of Tiranaral as I do."

CHAPTER 48

Outside Tamsyn's rooms at the Summer Court, Liam stood with his hand poised to knock on the door. He chewed distractedly on his lower lip. It was a cultural bloody nightmare. How was he supposed to know that showing grief, even speaking of the dead was such a taboo subject? And anyway, he'd only just found out about Vyvyan's passing for crying out loud. Surely Tamsyn would make allowances for that.

Vyvyan. A sick, empty feeling rose in his stomach and the pressure of fresh tears pushed at the back of his eyes. He swatted them away with the back of his fists. Fucking place! It felt so bloody wrong, forcing his feelings away like this.

From somewhere further along the corridor, the sound of children's laughter echoed. He dropped his hand back to his side.

That had been his third attempt at knocking.

He had absolutely no idea how bad his transgression had been. Kerenza seemed to understand, but, she had still warned him not to let his feelings show.

A night spent wandering between his bed and the balcony hadn't helped either. Each time he started to doze off, Liam became more and more convinced of what a prize arse he'd been. It'd serve him right if Tamsyn never wanted to see him again. She'd never understand, here in a world where grief was selfish. They were just too different, and he'd been a fool to think that there could ever be anything between them.

Crap, this was going nowhere, and standing out here worrying wasn't going to help. Liam knocked on the door. Long moments passed with no sound of activity from inside. He raised his hand to knock again, adrenaline making his muscles weak and jittery. The latch on the other side of the door clattered back and he swallowed hard, his mouth dry.

What if she shut the door in his face as soon as she saw him? What if she sent him away without giving him a chance to apologise? He had to speak first.

The door opened. She looked awful. Her lovely violet eyes were rimmed with red, and her hair was a tangled mess. She must've been up all night too. It was his fault; he'd done this. Tamsyn - light-hearted, loyal, and gloriously disrespectful, reduced to less than she deserved to be because of him. She was right; he really was a dumbass.

In retrospect, although he knew them to be her favourite, perhaps night lilies hadn't been such a good choice as a peace offering. When he'd picked them the previous evening, after his third of fourth trip to the balcony, they'd been in striking full bloom. Their star-shaped petals glowed faintly in the moonlight, and their dream-like fragrance made him question if he was even awake. Now, in the light of day, they were little more than a pathetic bunch of green stems. The ends swelled slightly where the flowers had closed, hiding from the harsh light of the sun. The whole sorry display was carefully gathered together with a bright red ribbon.

Inside her room at the Summer Court, Tamsyn stood and looked out at the man from another world. He twisted his feet nervously and his eyes were dark from lack of sleep. Most ridiculously of all, in his outstretched hand, he grasped a bouquet of night lilies. Night lilies - of all things! In full daylight! Nothing he might have said, could have expressed his lack of familiarity with the ways of Enys Avalen more eloquently.

Any uncertainty Tamsyn had felt through the previous evening and the long, long night fled in the presence of this man, who clearly had never meant any harm. She put her hand up in front of her face to suppress a laugh that was mostly pure relief and failed completely.

CHAPTER 49

Sunlight flashed, violet and peridot-green, from the mirror-like dragonflies hovering over the surface of the Summer Court plunge pool. Their wings blurred and smeared in the air.

Sitting between Kerenza and Tamsyn on one of the stone benches, Liam shook his head; the soft hum of the dragonflies' wings was getting into his head and making it hard to think. He shifted uncomfortably on the seat. Kerenza had called them here to discuss how to return the Soul to Lyskerrys. The last time they'd talked about it was when he'd learned of Vyvyan's death. They hadn't made a whole lot of progress on that occasion.

An eddy of cool mist blew from the waterfall, and Liam watched goose bumps form on Tamsyn's arms. He reached towards her but stopped himself. He'd felt this way before - back before all this had begun. Then, he'd been under the influence of Kerenza's beguilement and had been unable to think of anything else. He could've forgotten everything he loved in his own world and faded away, and to Kerenza, it would've been nothing.

It was different with Tamsyn. The desire grew stronger each time he was with her, and, actually, even when he wasn't, but it was still somewhat under his control. He wanted to warm her for her sake, not because of some nameless, haunting longing he couldn't even begin to understand. He reached out and rubbed her arm, she glanced over at him, smiled and mouthed: "Thank you."

"Oh, how lovely," said Kerenza disdainfully. "Since you two appear to have resolved your differences, and the Otherworlder has accepted that he is not, in fact, on the wrong timeline, perhaps we can return to the issue in hand. I believe that we got as far as you almost losing the Soul because of a simple evanescence charm."

"Kerenza!" Tamsyn chided. "We are all worried, but please let us not lose sight of the fact that Liam is trying to help us." Kerenza closed her eyes and pinched her brow for a second before beckoning to Liam to continue.

Liam took a steadying breath. "The person that stole the Soul, took a boat along the Ebronndir, all the way to the waterfall and then jumped off. That was when I realised he knew where the gateway was. He was going back to Tiranaral. Anyway, thing is, the reason no one could find the Soul was that once it was there, it transformed into an elderly lady. She, the Soul, was terrified."

Kerenza stood and walked towards the pool. She gazed out across the water and tapped the fingers of one hand against her lips. It was like she had forgotten Liam and Tamsyn were even there. "Yes, it makes sense. Some things cannot exist in the same way in different realities; the rules there will not allow it. Tiranaral would be unable to tolerate the Soul in its true form. It would be forced to transform. And of course, it would be frightened. So much of it would have no way to translate into that reality."

Liam coughed, and Kerenza turned back from the pool, blinking. "For what it's worth," he continued, "I also saw the thief. Close up. Really close up. And, well, the thing is…" Liam swallowed. The thief was one of his own, a human. What if Tamsyn held him responsible? What if she thought differently about him? "I, er… know who it is."

Kerenza tutted and widened her eyes at him. "And?"

"Peter, Peter Trevorrow. My best friend Jacob's dad. He's not one of you…"

Kerenza waved his concerns away. "It makes little difference at this stage. We just need to recover the Soul. Whatever your friend's father's reasons were, it sounds like things did not turn out the way he planned. We know the fate of the Soul, and you know how to find it in Tiranaral."

"There's more," Liam continued. "After the Soul transformed, she ran back to the gateway, back into the channel. I think she went even further back in time. But that doesn't matter right? She still exists in the present, so it must be okay. But as for getting her back…"

Kerenza turned to him, her brow drawn down. "You think that there could be problems?"

"Yeah," said Liam, "she'll be easy enough to find, but she won't come willingly. She won't communicate with anyone, it's like she's in her own world. If anyone tries to talk to her, she'll probably just ignore them. Except…"

"Except?" prompted Kerenza.

"Except for Jacob."

"The same Jacob? Your friend Jacob?" said Tamsyn.

"Yeah, but not how you think. He's the only person I've ever seen her react to, but she won't go near him, she's terrified of him. She's been like that around him for years…"

Tamsyn leaned forward, suddenly focussed. "Wait. That's it, your friend's father, don't you see? That's the connection, that's the reason the Soul acts differently around him."

"What? No, sorry, you've lost me," said Liam.

"Think about it, dumbass," Tamsyn was smiling broadly now, her eyes gleaming with excitement.

Liam smiled back; it was mostly relief. He had come so close to losing this with her. But he still had no idea what she was talking about.

"Look, how was Jacob's father able to take the Soul?" asked Tamsyn.

"What? We already know how he took it. I watched him do it. He sneaked into the Cathedral with an evanescence charm."

"And?" prompted Tamsyn.

"And... I still don't get it, sorry."

Kerenza look upwards and sighed. "I think what Tamsyn is trying, and failing miserably, to point out to you, is: how many people do you know from Tiranaral who make a habit of visiting the Cathedral? It is really not that complicated. Even for a human."

This was crazy, Tamsyn was making no sense, and Kerenza was just being... well, Kerenza. Obviously, no one from his world did that. They couldn't navigate the channel. Christ, they wouldn't even be able to find it... they... wait...

"His dad...?"

"Yes? Come on Liam, you have this, you are actually quite clever... for a human," said Tamsyn with a sharp glance at Kerenza.

"His dad must be a... drifter?"

"And drifting," Tamsyn finished for him triumphantly, "is passed down through families!"

"So, you're saying it's genetic, that Jacob could be one too?"

"I think it's almost a certainty," said Tamsyn. "It has to be the reason the Soul reacts to him and no one else."

Kerenza was suddenly very animated. "Yes, yes, of course, your friend." She was pacing briskly and chewing on her fingers. "His father cannot be trusted, drifter, or not. But your friend - there is a reason she reacts to him. She knows!" Kerenza strode back across the room and stopped in front of Liam. "You can persuade him!"

Liam's face dropped. "Like I said, it won't work, she won't go near him."

She grasped Liam's shoulders. "Yes, but that is because it does not understand. It is in a reality where it cannot exist as itself. The Soul is not just terrified of your friend, it is terrified of everything."

Kerenza's eyes were glittering, and she was trying to hide her smile behind her hand. She turned to Tamsyn. "The Soul is coming back! This is really it! The magic will return, and the city will heal." She steeped in close raising her arms as if she was going to embrace her, then dropped them to her sides. "Tamsyn, Lyskerrys will not be lost!"

"Yes… but there is still the matter of the ghost," cautioned Tamsyn.

Kerenza waved her concern away. "What can the ghost do - damage more fountains? With the Soul healing the city, it is merely an inconvenience. Lyskerrys will no longer be fading. We will have all the time in the world to deal with the ghost."

Then she was walking again and muttering to herself. "We still need to find a way to get her to trust him enough. All it would take is something… something to remind her of who she is." Again, she returned to Liam. "Assuming we can come up with something, would he do it? Would he bring her to the channel?"

"I'll ask," said Liam. "But he won't like it. His father caused the family a shedload of grief when he started saying he could travel to another reality. People really don't like to believe things like that in Tiranaral.

CHAPTER 50

Steam rolled across the low ceiling of Jacob's kitchen like time-lapsed storm clouds. The familiar creaking and bubbling sound of his discoloured old plastic jug-kettle filled the room with its reassuring presence. It was a brief return to normality amidst the strange events that pervaded their lives recently.

Jacob jammed a plastic milk bottle back into the fridge and nudged the door closed with his hip. "So, what is it you have to tell me this time? More about Lyskerrys I suppose." He held out a tannin stained mug towards Liam that proudly proclaimed, 'Gamers don't die – they respawn!' around the outside.

"Yeah, pretty much," said Liam, taking the mug.

"Well, get on with it then," said Jacob, lounging backwards against the worktop. He couldn't possibly be comfortable, but somehow, he made it look like he was.

"There're a few things, and they're gonna sound a bit weird."

Jacob slurped a mouthful coffee. "For Chrissakes Liam - the last thing you told me was that all the crap my dad had been spouting for years was true, and I dealt with that okay."

"What, when you punched me into a wall, you mean? You'll forgive me if I'm a bit cautious about giving you any more news."

Jacob flushed and looked at the floor.

Liam took a deep breath. "Okay, so to start off with, the problems in Lyskerrys are all linked. The place has what they call a Soul - had, I should say - it had a Soul. It's really important to them. Sort of like a god or a lifeforce. Anyway, it's been stolen, and everything's going to crap. That's why my girlf... my friend, Tamsyn was in trouble."

"friend?" Jacob said, looking up again.

"Yeah, whatever. Look, the point is, I now know who took it, and you're not going to like it."

Jacob closed his eyes and shook his head slowly. "Go on then, who took it?"

"Your dad," said Liam bluntly. "Sorry JJ, no kinder way to put it."

Jacob's gaze dropped to the floor again. "Figures. Do you happen to know why he took it?"

"Nope, 'fraid not."

"You said there were a few things."

"Yeah, well, he brought it back here. It's still here, that's why their whole world is dying. Anyway, it turns out the Soul can't exist in the same form here as does in the Otherworld. Something about magic and the laws of physics not playing nicely together, so it was forced to transform."

"Transform?" Jacob repeated.

"Into a bag-lady."

Jacob stopped with his mug midway to his mouth and raised his eyes from his coffee to look directly at Liam: "Seriously? A bag-lady? No, don't tell me, let me guess, the Queen of England, right?"

"Yep, ten XP to player number one!"

To Liam's surprise, his weak attempt at humour seemed to have worked, and Jacob smiled at him over the top of his coffee. "Well, just so long as you don't expect me to have anything to do with her. You know how she is around me."

"Yeah," said Liam, "the thing is..."

"Oh, no," said Jacob. "No fucking way, she literally freaks every time she sees me. You do know I had to hide from her when I woke up by the fountain a few nights ago, right?"

"Yeah, you told me. Look, we have to get her back to the Otherworld, and to do that we need your help. You're the only person who exists to her. I spoke with Tamsyn and Kerenza about it…"

"Kerenza?"

"She's like a high priestess. Well, she is now anyway..." Liam turned away and gazed out of the kitchen window.

Jacob set his coffee down on the worktop and took a step towards Liam. "Mate, you okay?"

"Yeah, yeah," said Liam turning back to face Jacob, and rubbing his eyes with the back of his hand, "I'm fine. It's a long story. Anyway, Tamsyn and Kerenza think the reason the Queen reacts to you the way she does is because she's aware of your dad's connection to the Otherworld. Not in any way she understands – but she senses something. They believe that another connection to her home might be enough to get through to her. It's got to be you mate, no one else even exists to her."

Jacob slumped down onto a chair and rested his head in his hands. "Christ, I don't know man."

Liam dragged another chair over and sat next to him. "Look mate, you feel bad because of what your dad did – I get it – but we still need to get the Soul back. Return the Soul and you wipe the slate clean. What do you say? Wanna do something about it?" Liam opened his palm to reveal a dull metal disc about the size of a coin.

Jacob glanced at it then rolled his eyes. "What the hell is that supposed to be?"

"This, my friend, is an evanescence charm."

"Am I supposed to be impressed? It doesn't look like much."

"Oh," said Liam, "you'd be surprised."

CHAPTER 51

"Remind me again why this a good idea, Liam. She's literally going to freak the fuck out as soon as she sees me. I'm not even joking." Jacob kicked miserably at an imaginary stone as he and Liam waited on the opposite side of the road to the fountain.

"Come on JJ, we've been through this. It'll be fine."

Easy for him to say. He wasn't the one everyone was going to be staring at when the Queen of England started shrieking. And it wasn't like she ever hurt anyone, well, not unless you were including hearing damage. She didn't deserve any of this. No, this was all on Jacob.

"Look man," said Liam, "I've seen how you look at her. I know you want what's best for her, despite what anyone else might think. If we can do this, she'll be home. She can't be happy here."

"S'pose," said Jacob, "but people are going to notice, aren't they? I mean, if we do get her back to the Otherworld. They'll be asking where she's gone."

"I dunno, they don't seem too bothered to me. I haven't seen too many of them actually trying to help her out, have you? In fact, the only person I've ever seen do that is you."

Jacob stopped kicking and looked up at Liam. "Meaning?"

"Do you think I don't know it's been you leaving bags of chips out by the fountain for her?"

Crap, he'd seen that? Jacob had been so careful. It wasn't much as far as making up for shouting at her went, but well, it wasn't like there was a whole lot else he could do.

"Look Liam, don't tell anyone, okay? It's just... I dunno, I kind of..."

"Don't worry, your secret's safe with me. Anyway, there's no sign of her, it could be ages before she shows up." Liam nodded towards the baker's shop on the other side of the road. "Want a pasty while we wait?"

That was a bit more like it, they'd skipped breakfast this morning so they could be sure of being at the fountain before the Queen turned up, and Jacob's stomach was starting to notice. "Always got room for a pasty, long as you're paying, obviously."

"Okay, wait here. Someone needs to be around in case she arrives. And you'd better take this." Liam dropped the chain of the evanescence charm over Jacob's head. "You might need it."

Jacob took hold of the charm and lifted it up to his face. "hmmm, let's hope not." Liam smiled and wandered over to the road to wait for a gap in the traffic. "Grab us a coffee, will you?" Jacob called after him.

They nearly missed the Queen when she arrived.

"JJ," hissed Liam.

"What?" replied Jacob through a mouthful of pastry, as he gazed down at his phone screen.

"Get off your phone. Down at the end of the road, it's the Queen."

Jacob looked up, his eyebrows disappearing up inside his beanie hat. "Shit. Look, are you sure this is going to work?"

"Nope, but it's the only option we've got. Come on, let's go."

Reluctantly, Jacob trailed Liam across the road, arriving well before the Queen. "Stay behind the fountain, just in case the charm only works at close range here. We don't want her running off before we get near to her. I'll let you know when she's close."

"You probably won't need to," said Jacob, ducking around to the back of the fountain, putting it between him and the Queen, "I'm bound to hear her muttering."

For a few moments the only sounds were the rumble of passing cars, the chattering of shoppers and the trickle of water from the fountain. Soon another noise joined them - the clack, clack, clacking of a single shopping trolley wheel as it tried to steer in a different direction to the other three.

"Jacob, now!"

Shit - here goes nothing. With his heart thumping in his ears Jacob stepped out from behind the fountain, straight into the path of the Queen of England. The Queen's eyes opened wide in her wrinkled, wind-burned face as he appeared in front of her. For the first time Jacob really noticed her eyes, they weren't blue at all, not really, they were a brilliant turquoise.

She was so close that he could see the fine network of red capillaries that laced her cheeks and nose. God, here we go. Jacob gritted his teeth and screwed his eyes together. There was bound to be screeching, and after that, probably crying as well.

Silence.

More silence.

Jacob half-opened an eye and risked a sideways glance, teeth still clamped together in readiness.

Instead of running, the Queen just stood there staring. A thin, trembling, liver-spotted hand reached out towards him. What the hell was she doing? In his peripheral vision Liam was holding out his hands, fingers spread wide, imploring him to stay calm. Really? The Queen of England was reaching for his throat, and that was the best Liam could come up with.

With hurried, rodent-like movements, the Queen started scratching at Jacob's neck. He froze, eyes wide and mouth open. Shit! This was worse than the screaming, at least he knew what she was doing when she was screaming. Liam hissed from over by the fountain. "JJ! The charm, show her the charm!"

Jacob grabbed at the zip of his hoodie. The Queen's eyes widened, and her whole body tensed. She stopped moving. No, no, don't scream, please don't scream. Come on JJ, calm it down, don't blow it now. "Okay," he said, "It's okay… you just carry on, don't mind me. I'm not even here…" Very slowly he lowered his hands, allowing her to resume her search. The Queen relaxed and reached out to Jacob's neck again. Grasping the zipper, she yanked it down, exposing the charm.

Jacob's mouth dropped open. He risked a quick glance over to Liam. Liam grinned back. At the Queen's touch, the evanescence charm responded with soft frills of aquamarine that danced and skittered around the edges of its worn inscriptions.

Closing her eyes, the Queen of England lifted the evanescence charm, still looped by its chain around Jacob's neck, and placed it lovingly against her cheek. Little trails of phosphoresce followed her tears as they ran across its surface.

The Queen of England looked up, and for the first time that anyone could remember, focussed directly on the person in front of her. "Home?" She asked.

"Home," replied Jacob, "Yeah, let's get you home."

CHAPTER 52

An elbow dug into Jacob's ribs, and he blinked up from his phone screen. "What?"

Liam nodded forwards, widening his eyes meaningfully.

Sitting on a bench further along the road was Davy. Crap. Couldn't anything be simple? All they needed to do was walk the Queen back to Jacob's flat. From there it was only a short drive to Lamellion and the gateway.

"Fuck." said Jacob. The Queen slapped his hand. "Ow! Sorry, Okay, I get it - you don't like swearing - Jesus."

Liam smirked. "At least he's on his own. He might leave us alone."

"Some chance of that, he probably still hasn't forgiven us for ruining his chances with those girls."

Suddenly, the Queen was on the move, running off ahead of them and veering out into the road. She was heading towards the bench. Davy was on his feet.

"Shit! Come on Liam." Jacob broke into a trot and followed, dodging cars as he ran across the road.

Liam caught up moments later. "Bloody hell, she's faster than she looks, isn't she?"

Jacob was staring ahead. "What the..."

The Queen had stopped in front of Davy and was searching through his jacket pockets.

"Alright Ena!" said Davy, he was laughing and squirming about as if she was tickling him. "Okay, okay, just wait a minute, I've got something." He reached into an inside pocket, pulled out a sweet, and pressed it into the Queen's hand. She beamed up at him, trilling contentedly.

Liam turned to Jacob. "What the hell? What did he just call her?"

"Sounded like 'Ena'. I never even knew she had a name - how come he knows it?"

The Queen popped the sweet into her mouth before meticulously re-folding the wrapper and putting it back into Davy's pocket.

Jacob gripped Liam's forearm. "What. The. Actual. Fuck. Am I looking at?"

"No idea mate," said Liam, "and close your mouth, you look like an idiot."

Davy glared up, noticing them for the first time. "What?" he snapped. "Not everyone treats me like you lot did at school you know." Then his face softened, and he smiled down at the Queen again. "So, you gonna find it today Ena?"

"Oh yes dearie. Yes, we are most certainly going to find it today."

"Fuck me!" said Davy, looking back at Liam and Jacob. "She's never said that before."

The Queen slapped him across the chest.

Davy grinned. "Sorry Ena"

***

Jacob slammed the door of his battered old Volkswagen Polo and leaned back against it shaking his head. Even though he'd seen it before, the thought of Liam and the Queen stepping down into the stream still seemed like a bloody ridiculous idea.

He wandered over the little concrete footbridge and looked down into the water. "So, it's right here then, is it?" It didn't look like it was right here. It didn't look like there was anything right here other than a sad looking stream.

"Oh, it's here," replied Liam. "It's quite beautiful really."

Jacob pulled off his beanie hat and ran his hand through his hair. "And she's really, you know, going - for good like?"

It was going to be weird not having her around. She'd always been there, and he should know, he'd spent much of his life trying to avoid her. He wouldn't need to leave chips out for her at the fountain anymore. Over the years it'd become a bit of a ritual, and it made him feel a bit better about himself too. What was he going to do now? Still, if what Liam said was true - and it was looking like it was, what with people vanishing into rivers and glowing necklaces - then she'd be better off there.

Liam wandered over, leading the Queen of England by the hand. He stood next to Jacob and leaned back against the handrail. "Time to say your goodbyes mate. It feels like the gateway's about to move on."

Shit, he should say something, but what? How do you talk to someone who until today had only ever screamed at you? Jacob turned to face the Queen. "Look, I er... the thing is... I've been meaning to say..."

The Queen let go of Liam's hand and stepped over to Jacob, stopping right in front him. She was tiny, actually, when she was this close. She'd always been this huge presence in his life, but there was nothing to her. Jacob looked down into those unusual turquoise eyes. Her fingers brushed over his shoulders, pulling, plucking, and tidying. Then she put something into his pocket and pressed his hand over the top of it.

"Little help here," called Liam. He was already knee-deep in the stream.

"Come on then Ena," said Jacob, "let's get you home." He took the Queen's hand and helped her down the steep bank into the stream.

Moments later Liam and the Queen of England were lost to view as a waterspout swirled up around them. There was a flash of bright turquoise light from the evanescence charm, and the vortex spun itself away to nothing more than a few ribbons of gravity defying water, and then they too were gone.

Jacob slipped and stumbled his way back up to the roadside. Once there, he reached into his pocket, his fingers closing around the small object he found inside. He pulled his hand out and looked own at a grimy, plastic chip-fork.

"Fuck," he said, wiping his eyes with the back of his other hand.

CHAPTER 53

Nothing had changed.

The Queen of England still stood beside Liam, holding his hand. The same bird-bright eyes still peered out from the same wind-burnt and wizened face, just as they did when they entered the channel.

Nothing had changed, but some intangible part of her radiated out across the universe.

Nothing had changed, but the Queen was her past, her present and her future all at once. She was all that she had ever been and all the that she ever would be. Time dissolved in her presence. And she didn't just transcend time, the Soul extended into dimensions that Liam could not even fully comprehend.

Nothing had changed.

But everything was different.

Liam opened his mouth and tried to speak, but there were no words. The Queen was so much more than she had been a moment before. He could see it all now, the Soul was Lyskerrys and Lyskerrys was the Soul. They were different aspects of the same thing, and one could not exist without the other. No wonder Lyskerrys was fading without her, there was no other way it could be.

Taking his free hand in hers, the Queen smiled. Liam was vaguely aware of an aura of aquamarine suffusing the air around them, of brilliant points of light, buffeting against each other. But that was merely physical. The Soul blew through him like a summer wind, scattering him like pollen. The light seared across sensory boundaries like they simply didn't exist. He could feel it, he could hear it, he could taste it.

Across a thousand years and a thousand miles, and as soft as a whisper in the space between heartbeats, there was a word.

Breathe.

In a single inhalation Liam breathed in the whole world. And when he breathed out again, he and the Soul were one.

He was connected to everything.

Everything.

Everywhere.

From the ancient paths of the stars, etched into the dark glass of the night, to the lifetimes between galaxies. From the secret currents of the Ebronndir, to the long, slow descent of ocean silt, falling as soft as ash. He was the warmth of sunlight, the glorious night, and the crystal sea.

Somewhere, he was crying. But in whatever place those tears flowed there was no embarrassment and there was no shame. This was a wonder that couldn't be encompassed by mere words, it was a religious experience. No one could feel this and react in any other way. No one could feel this and ever be the same again.

And when he was just a man once more, standing at the base of the Ana, he knew that he was also a part of something greater than himself.

In his hand Liam held a glowing aquamarine about the size of an apple. The Queen was gone. The Queen was everywhere. And the Soul of Lyskerrys was home.

CHAPTER 54

As Kerenza carried the Soul into the chamber, the worn carvings appeared to lean out of the walls as the bobbing sphere of light passed by. She allowed herself a smile. It mattered not that Liam had never particularly liked her - not in the way he liked Tamsyn and Vyvyan. Poor Vyvyan; constantly agonising over whether asking the Otherworlder to help was the right thing to do. Kerenza had always known he would be equal to the task, and he had proved her right. But supposing she had been wrong, should they have allowed Lyskerrys to fail rather than take that chance? Of course not! The Soul had been lost, afraid, and in the wrong world. Someone had to act, and none of the others were prepared to put aside their emotions and do what was required. So, in a way, she had made sacrifices too. Not that anyone would see it that way, and not that it really mattered. She did hope Liam would eventually understand though. She had grown to rather like him.

As she neared the centre of the chamber, the lonely clicking of Kerenza's sandals was joined by a gentle gurgling.

The water surrounding the cupola began to fluoresce, building upwards upon itself in collapsing bursts. Kerenza drew in a slow, deep breath. There had been a time when she never would have thought this possible. A time when she was convinced that Lyskerrys would become another lost city.

As she placed the Soul on the plinth, the curtains of water reached the roof of the cupola; the reverse waterfall was flowing once again. Soul-light sparkled through the water, casting tendrils and beads of aquamarine light across the cavern walls. Kerenza inhaled, breathing in the world; the Soul of Lyskerrys was back. She had done what was needed. Brushing her fingers slowly across the Soul, she turned away and walked back across the chamber.

Something knocked into her legs. Whatever it was, she felt it overbalance and reached forward to catch it. Her fingers brushed past cold metal a fraction of a second too late. The familiar sound of shattering glass rang through the silence. Water washed over her feet. A night lily planter? How did she miss it? It had been right in front of her.

Kerenza peered down, but she could see nothing. But it had to be there, she had heard it fall. She swished her foot through the spilt water, and the bright ring of broken glass reached her ears. The hair on the back of her neck stood on end. Slowly, Kerenza turned around. It could not to be true.

She strained her eyes and peered across the chamber; the cupola was gone, but there was a faint glimmer, just a wavering smear of grey. Adrenaline twisted her stomach, she was going to vomit, fighting her instinct to run, she waded through a sea of dread back to the middle of the room. Her hands trembled as she gathered up the Soul and turned to the door. Within a few steps she was completely lost. Where… where was the door? She was breathing too fast, becoming light-headed. Her thoughts came slow and sluggish. On shaking legs, Kerenza inched blindly forward across the chamber. One arm was outstretched in front of her, the Soul grasped close to her in the other. Nothing. There was nothing there but empty space. And then, suddenly, stone beneath her fingers. Scrabbling her hands across its surface, she searched for a familiar pattern, a candle holder, anything. If she could just find something she recognised, something to tell her where she was. Her breath was loud in her ears, how could she have become so lost?

The sound was almost imperceptible at first. Kerenza held her breath and stained to hear. Had she imagined it? But when it came again, there was no mistake: the long drawn out 'ahhh' of a final breath. Her skin prickled. She could almost imagine words, it almost sounded like... No, that was ridiculous. "Kereeeeenzaaa". The room seemed to collapse around her, concentrating the sound into a death rattle. "Kerenzaaaaaaah". She sunk to the floor, clasping the Soul to her breast and whimpering. It could not end like this - not after all the Soul had endured.

Kerenza forced herself back to her feet, feeling her way up the wall. She was High Priestess now; it would *not* end this way. Beneath her foot something crunched and shattered. The broken planter! The room rotated wildly in her mind as recognition flashed from synapse to synapse. She was nowhere near where she thought she was. She froze - the room was suddenly silent; there was nothing but her breathing, loud in her head. It had heard her! For a moment the darkness contracted. It was all she needed. Across the chamber was the faintest glow of light. The door!

The ghost billowed outward, filling the room and roaring like an inferno. Kerenza launched herself forward, sprinting blindly towards her memory of the door. But in that brief glimpse there had been something else, a shadow, a chaise longue. She swerved left, felt it brush against her leg. The ground dropped away. Kerenza's foot jolted down into one of the channels. She was out and moving again before the water even began to soak through her shoe. But she had definitely done some damage. The crackling, snapping sound boiled around her like a living thing. Again, and again she slammed her free hand against the wall, searching for the door, but pain exploded across her back, taking her legs out from under her. She fell hard, her head smashing into a stone step.

Was that really her head? It felt so distant - more like a soft jolt than the pain of hard, unforgiving stone. Little points and tails of light wriggled in front of her eyes. Oh dear, that was probably not a good sign. Probably not a good sign at all. Still, at least that awful noise was subsiding, and the floor was surprisingly soft and warm. The darkness closed in around her. It was not so terrifying now.

As her eyes fluttered closed, the last thing Kerenza saw was a softly glowing aquamarine laying on the floor beside her. It really was rather lovely.

CHAPTER 55

A word here, a touch there, following the threads that wove all things together, she found pathways through space and through time. She made the jumps, flashing from synapse to synapse, memory to memory, and place to place, faster and faster and further and further back.

Thoughts and ideas, personalities and places, connection after connection, linking one after another, they all streaked past, twisting and bucking at dizzying speed, until she began to lose track of where she was.

Too fast!

The links were being made too fast.

Connections raced past almost before she was aware of them. What if she missed one? She could ricochet off to the wrong place, the wrong time. But somewhere within she knew - she just had to let go and allow the part of her that understood this chaos to navigate.

The connections pitched and swerved, blurred and coalesced, until they flowed together into one line, a solitary path, leading back and back and back to a single event.

In an age before memory, a blade was forged - a blade so sharp that it could cut through time.

Vyvyan was the breath in the bellows that drove the forge towards white heat, and the murmuration of sparks that twisted and rolled from the furnace. She was the sweat on the brow of the swordsmith, and the ringing of the hammer as it struck again and again drawing out the blade. She was the secret of forging and folding and forging and folding again until frost ferns bloomed across the metal.

She was the scalding clouds of steam as the sword was quenched at the very moment of the solstice. She was the skittering and popping of beads of superheated water, scattering across the blade. She was the white hot and the cherry red and the peacock-feather blue of its cooling.

She boiled as acid over its surface raising the ferns still further from the face of the metal, and she glinted in the starlight that caught the impossibly thin edge of the Solstice Blade.

She was misty rain lashing through a deserted car park in the world of men.

And snow in Cornwall.

And the malevolent trick that secreted a blade in the pocket of a teenage boy, excited by the prospect of snow.

She was biting pain in a frozen palm.

And now she was Liam.

Liam's eyes flashed open.
He knew.
He knew Kerenza was in trouble.
He knew she was in the Cathedral.
He knew the ghost was closing in on her.
He knew it was Vyvyan who had told him.

And he knew something about the ghost that he should've seen all along.

In a single movement he was sitting up in bed. He had to move fast. "Tamsyn," he hissed. She didn't answer. "Tamsyn!" The bedclothes next to him undulated and mumbled. A tangle of brown hair slithered back under the covers. "Tamsyn, wake up!" Tamsyn stretched cat-like beneath the sheets before the covers were unceremoniously flung forward. There was a waft of stale perfume.

"What?"

"It's Kerenza! The ghost - it's trapped her in the Cathedral with the Soul!" Liam jumped out of bed, stumbling into his discarded jeans and dragging them up around his waist.

Tamsyn was instantly awake and sitting up. "What? But that can't be! The ghost only attacks the fountains."

"I know, I know." Liam's voice was muffled by his faded t-shirt as he fought to pull it over his head. "Tamsyn, it's Jacob. The ghost is Jacob. He must've fallen asleep. I've got to get back and wake him."

"But... but, how can you know?"

"The Soul told me." Liam turned to run towards the door.

"Wait," called Tamsyn, "how will you find him in time."

"Don't worry," Liam called over his shoulder as he clattered and slipped back down the stairs, "I know where he'll be. Just get to Kerenza. Get to the Soul. Make sure they're safe. And take care."

Liam raced up the stairs from the Pipe Well. His journey through the channel had lasted an eternity, and all that time Kerenza was trapped with the ghost. The fountain was only about one hundred yards away, but it was nearly all uphill.

He tore around the corner onto Pike Street at the base of the guildhall clock tower.

Fifty yards to go.

At the top of the hill, the sour glare of the lamp on the fountain burned away the soft edges of the encroaching night.

Jacob was nowhere to be seen.

Liam's mind was racing. If anything happened to Kerenza or the Soul, his best friend would be unknowingly responsible. Jacob would never forgive himself. Liam wasn't sure he would be able to either.

The steep incline, his distraction, and blind panic were conspiring to slow him down. His breath was already coming to him in deep laboured gasps. The metallic tang of blood filled his mouth. He was going to pay for this. He put everything he had into pounding up the hill. He had never run so hard in his life, but his progress was impossibly slow.

For God's sake! Come on! Running in a swimming pool would have been easier.

Finally, he crested the top of the hill and scanned anxiously across the road to the fountain.

Nothing.

Where the hell was Jacob? He had to be here! It was the only thing that made any sense. Jacob was the ghost; he must have been sleepwalking again.

Liam sprinted across the road, grabbed hold of the shaped granite trough that was blocking his view, and pivoted himself towards the fountain. And there, laying on the ground, just where he knew he had to be, was the curled-up form of Jacob.

"Jacob!" he screamed as loud as he could with the last of the breath he had remaining in his lungs. "Wake up!"

Jacob mumbled and rolled away to face the fountain, trying to pull the corner of his jacket around him as if it was a duvet, but not before Liam noticed the strange smile on his face. This was not Jacob's usual easy smile, this was altogether more sinister, more vengeful.

As he slid to a halt at the foot of the fountain, one of Liam's feet accidentally connected with Jacob's exposed back. Jacob grunted and curled up into an even tighter ball.

"Jacob!" screamed Liam again, bending down and grabbing the collar of his jacket and shaking it furiously.

Jacob's eyes snapped open, wide with terror. Still dreaming-drunk, he tried to scramble away, staring wildly around at things only he could see and waving his arms in front of his face.

Liam shook him again: "Jacob, wake up!"

Jacob blinked. The panicked expression left his face to be replaced by one of confusion. "Alright! Alright, for Chrissakes Liam what's the matter with you? I'm awake, okay? I'm awake."

Liam could almost see the ruins of Jacob's dream collapsing in his eyes as his expression of confusion was replaced with one of shock. "Oh fuck!" he muttered, "I've been sleepwalking again."

Liam stood over him with his hands on his knees wheezing noisily after his furious run up the hill. "Yeah, unfortunately that's not all."

CHAPTER 56

On his way to answer the front door Jacob paused to glance in the mirror. Even in the dimness of the hallway he looked terrible; the combination of anxiety and sleep deprivation had left him with a fine sheen of sweat glistening over waxy skin. Dark shadows hung below his half-lidded eyes.

Judging by the reaction, he didn't look too good to Liam either. Jacob stood back to let his friend enter. "You took your time. I've literally been freaking out here on my own."

"Whoa, calm down mate." Liam held two takeaway coffees out to Jacob. "Peace offering. Come and sit down a minute. We need to talk."

Jacob took the cups. "Bloody right we do. You tell me I'm the ghost, and I've attacked someone in a cathedral, then fuck off back to the Otherworld with nothing more than a warning not to fall asleep. Which, incidentally, I did completely on trust, because that's the kind of bloke I am, and now I'm knackered and out of coffee and the best you can say is *calm down mate.*"

Jacob led the way into the sitting room, nodded at the sofa and held one of the cups out to Liam.

"They're both yours," said Liam, "I figured two double espressos should do it." He gathered a pile of game boxes from the couch and dropped them onto the table. "I see you've been busy while I've been gone."

"What? I had to do something while I was waiting for you, didn't I? So, what's the news?" said Jacob, waving the remote at the television to switch it off as he slumped into his chair.

"Well," said Liam, "first off, the soul breathers know what's going on and they know how to fix it, so you can relax."

Jacob downed his first espresso in two gulps, then leaned forward in his chair, looking up at Liam with a deeply furrowed brow. "What about what's-her-name. You said I…"

"Kerenza, and she's fine. Tamsyn found her collapsed on the floor of the Cathedral…"

"Collapsed? How the hell can she be fine if she'd collapsed?"

"She's got a sore back and a bump on the head. She'll be back to her old self in no time."

Some of the tension left Jacob's face. "Right, well now you're back, I suppose this must be the part where you tell me just what the hell is going on and just what the hell you propose to do about it."

"Okay, okay. The soul breathers tell me that you were attacking the gateways in your dreams because you see Lyskerrys as the reason your father left. Destroy the gateways and the problem goes away."

"Yes, but…"

"Hang, on stay with me. But then other people started leaving you for Lyskerrys." Liam pointed at himself. "I present Exhibit A." Jacob rolled his eyes, but Liam just grinned and continued. "Targeting the gateways obviously wasn't enough to prevent that, so you started targeting the people who were involved."

"Do you have to keep saying you? It's not like I was doing it on purpose."

"Sorry mate. It really is okay, no one blames you."

"So, how did you know it was me?"

"I was starting to put it together, but the really weird thing was…"

"really weird? As opposed to what - regular weird?"

Liam smiled. "As I was saying, the really weird thing was that the Soul told me. I think it happened because Vyvyan is with the Soul, and Vyvyan and I had a connection. It all kind of links up. Anyway, the hauntings all coincided with when you were asleep under the fountain."

Jacob swallowed the last of his second espresso and put the cup down on the coffee table. "You said they know how to fix it."

"Yeah. Vyvyan was able to connect to my mind because she was high priestess. Well, now Kerenza's high priestess, she can do the same, and now the Soul's back she can direct it to where you need healing."

"Wait, you're going to let Kerenza do a bloody mind-job on me? But, she's the one that, you know, I did the thing to, in the place?"

"Exactly," said Liam, "and you really don't want to keep her waiting."

Jacob shook his head. "No, no, something's still not right, you're still overlooking one thing."

"Which is?" said Liam.

"I can't get there can I? I can't use the gateways. I can't travel through the scary-river-thing."

"The channel? Yeah, there is that," said Liam.

God, he could be seriously irritating when he wanted to be. "And?" said Jacob.

"And," Liam repeated with a slight smile, "there does appear to be a genetic component to this travelling-between-worlds business."

A genetic component - what the fuck was that supposed to mean? That you were born with it? That it was passed down to you? That was ridiculous. To be born with it he'd have to have... inherited it... from... someone...

Jacob looked Liam directly in the eye, and slowly stood up. "My bloody dad! He must have been able to get through to take the Soul in the first place! You're saying I can do it too?"

Liam leaned back on the coach and lifted his feet onto the coffee table. "Yeah, well, in theory. I mean, you'll probably be crap at it, but I can teach you."

Jacob whipped his beanie hat off his head and threw it at Liam, who rolled to one side, easily avoiding it.

Liam laughed. "What? Well, come on, how do you think you have been getting there in your sleep? Most people's dreams don't have an effect on the real world, do they?"

"Oh, I don't know," said Jacob. "I can think of at least one other person."

CHAPTER 57

Jacob shook his head and slowly ran a hand through his lank black hair. The action dislodged his beanie hat, which fell to the ground. He left it where it fell and snapped his mouth closed. He must look like some kind of idiot standing here gawping. But, bloody hell, this was impossible. His mouth fell slowly open again.

He and Liam were on a quayside beside a river. The lilac water was as clear as glass and flowed like silk. Where the river deepened it transitioned into a mysterious lavender. A gust of wind frosted the surface with a thousand hard edged ripples.

Out on the river a sleek vessel sliced through the water, sails flying high ahead of it like kites. People chatted and laughed on the deck, tending to the lines. Some of them were brightly dressed, and some of them weren't even people.

Away from the river graceful white stone and glass buildings arched upwards towards the sun, and in the distance obsidian mountains sliced the high clouds into rippling streamers.

Liam had told him what to expect before they had stepped into the water of the Pipe Well, but those had just been words. He hadn't believed him. Well he had, but not really. He believed that Liam believed it. But he'd still felt a bit of a twat as the water soaked into his training shoes. He'd heard similar words before of course, from his father, and he hadn't believed those either. Those words had destroyed his family and had been ammunition to Davy and Beckerleg and the customers in the pub. But this was real. It was actually real. All this time, all those years, it had been here, exactly as his dad had described it.

Relief flooded through him as tension he didn't even realise he had been holding onto melted away. Vertigo tilted the world beneath him, and Jacob sank down onto the ground. Even once he was sitting, he still had to support himself with a hand in the road on either side. This was so completely different to anything he'd ever known that it made his head spin. It made the whole world spin - whatever world it might be.

Jacob laughed, raising a hand to his mouth, and then quickly placed it back down again before he toppled over. Christ, he had some making up to do, but how the hell was anyone supposed to believe that something like this could be real?

Liam grinned down at him offering his hand. "Cool, isn't it?"

"Cool? For fuck's sake Liam, I don't know what this is, but it's way beyond cool."

Liam pulled Jacob to his feet. "Come on, you're getting in the way." A clattering noise on the road behind him caused Jacob to turn and look round. A man with flowing brown hair and legs like a horse, trotted past, and continued on up the road.

"Wait! That guy... was he a centaur?"

"A centaur?" said Liam. "Of course not, that would be ridiculous - centaurs have four legs."

CHAPTER 58

The sun was a vast wavering sphere low in the west, as Liam and Kerenza made their way to where Tamsyn and Jacob awaited them at The Autumn Sky. Above them a flight of evening swallows climbed and rolled higher and higher as if chasing the last fading rays of the sun in the afterglow of the day. Folding their wings in close to their bodies, the swallows plummeted earthward. At the last instant, they pulled out of their headlong plunge to swoop low over the Ebronndir, carving fine lines into the still surface of the river.

"Summer is coming to an end and all this will change you know," said Kerenza.

"Change?" replied Liam. "Change how?"

"Lyskerrys is not like your world. The Summer Court is not so called because it is only used in the summer. It's because of how it is in the summer. In the autumn it will be a different place, and in the winter; different again. The whole of Enys Avalen changes with the seasons."

"I suppose that's why it looks so different to how it did when I was here before, Christ! That seems like a lifetime ago."

"I expect so. Things are a lot more fluid here than in Tiranaral," she continued. "In your world, from one season to the next, even from one year to the next the buildings, the landscape, everything, remains the same. Here the city will change in tune with the seasons."

"I don't know how you can manage if the city keeps changing around you."

Kerenza laughed. "It is not so hard to understand; it is just nature. The weather changes, the trees and plants lose their leaves in Autumn and grow more in Spring, the length of the day and night change. You do not really notice, you just adapt."

Crossing over the bridge where he had stopped with Vyvyan on his first full evening in Lyskerrys, Kerenza halted.

She turned away and gazed out over the river. "Liam, before, when the Soul was missing… I…"

She spoke so quietly that it would have been easy not to hear her, if he didn't want to, if it let her keep her dignity.

"You may not like how I was, I may not have liked it, but someone had to…"

"Sorry, what?" said Liam, "I was miles away…"

"Oh, nothing, nothing important." Kerenza turned back to face him. "Is something wrong? You look… distant."

"No, nothing's wrong," he replied. "It's just that this place is so incredible, I can see why you were so desperate not to lose it."

"You have a life and family in Tiranaral. It's easy for your people to lose sight of that when they are here. It's one of the reasons why you have to forget."

"Yeah," said Liam, "I know, but I've never been good with endings."

Now the Soul was back, now the mystery of the ghost was solved, and now Lyskerrys was safe, Liam's time in Enys Avalen was drawing towards its end. They couldn't allow him to remember. No one ever remembered. But this was different, wasn't it? He hadn't asked for any of this, Kerenza had sought him out, Vyvyan had entered his mind, they had shared everything. And then there was Tamsyn. Kerenza was right, he did have a life and family in Tiranaral, but what he had here was family too. But no one ever remembered, did they?

It probably didn't matter that much anyway. You don't miss what you never had, and if he had no recollection of being here, wasn't that the same thing? But, if he was going forget, he was damned well going to make it count, whatever that was worth. He would live these last few precious hours in Lyskerrys to the full, even if he'd never know it.

Kerenza touched his arm. "I could, you know, beguile you. If it would make it easier... only if you wanted." Liam smiled to himself. That must be the first time she had ever actually asked him if it was okay.

"I'll be fine," he said, "but thank you. Really." Turning away from the view along the Ebronndir, they began the descent to the other side of the river.

Eventually Liam began to recognise buildings and taverns familiar to him from the night he and Tamsyn got drunk on storm-chasers. Soon he could see light spilling out of The Autumn Sky onto the street. In the doorway was the unmistakable figure of Tamsyn. Standing next to her with a broad grin on his face and bouncing on his toes even more than usual was Jacob.

Motioning to Jacob to wait at the door, Tamsyn skipped along the street towards them. Forcing herself playfully between Liam and Kerenza, she linked arms with them both. As they walked back towards Jacob and the tavern, Liam found his spirits lifting. It was curiously similar to the way a group of friends would act on a night out in his own world. Strange how amongst all the differences there is always something that makes us the same.

Liam's heart lurched again, this all felt so natural. He forced a smile onto his face. It wasn't as hard as he expected; Tamsyn had a way of making joy easy. "Your friend Jacob seems to like it here," she said, "and he certainly makes friends easily."

Liam smiled. "Oh yes, he does have a way with people."

"We had to step out for a breath of fresh air, he's worn himself out dancing."

"Dancing? You're joking, aren't you? I don't think I can ever remember him dancing before."

Jacob bounced over and slapped Liam on the back in greeting. "Man, you have got to hear the music here." He was flushed and breathing heavily, "And I don't mean just what they're playing, not that it's not utterly mind-blowing, but just music itself here, in this place, it's something else."

"Enjoying yourself then?" said Liam, smiling.

Jacob grabbed Liam's arm and dragged him towards the door.

"She hasn't been plying you with storm-chasers, has she?" asked Liam.

"Not yet," said Tamsyn, cuffing Liam across the shoulder, "but there's still time for that."

"Storm-chasers?" asked Jacob.

"Don't worry," said Liam. "Judging by how much you seem to be enjoying Lyskerrys, I think you're going to love them."

"Come on," said Jacob, pulling Kerenza towards him, "I want to dance." Liam stared after them in amazement - that must have been some mind connection she'd performed on Jacob. Tamsyn pulled on his arm, and together they followed Jacob and Kerenza into The Autumn Sky.

Inside, The Sky was a riot of laughter and noise. Since the restoration of the Soul the magic had returned to Lyskerrys and everyone in the tavern was taking full advantage. In place of the more usual candles, illumination was provided by ribbons of coloured light that flowed and twisted through the air. Across the room a group of musicians were preparing to play, and people were gathering in front of the stage.

"You weren't joking about the dancing," said Liam nodding in the direction that Jacob had disappeared with Kerenza. "Honestly, I have never seen him so..."

Before he could finish speaking, one of the musicians drew a long mournful note from a bowed, violin-like instrument, introducing the next song. The hum of the crowd dropped to nothing as everyone turned to face the stage. Anticipation filled the air. Frisson, amplified to levels he had never before experienced, shivered along the back of Liam's neck, raising hairs and inducing an almost trance-like sensation. It was the first time he had heard music here, and it was astonishing. That one note carried within it everything he loved about Lyskerrys and conveyed in its single, wavering, heart-breaking sound an entire chord. It was coloured with the scent of the night, the roar of the sea and enormity of the sky. But it was nothing compared to the sound of the full band as the rest of the musicians joined in.

Each note added was richer, more perfect and more evocative than anything Liam had ever known.

Tamsyn grabbed Liam's hand and dragged him out into the dance. Joy flowed through him as he gave himself over to the incredible music. He was passed from partner to partner as the music swelled until it was his whole world. A wild parade of faces passed by as he was whirled around the room. At one point, he couldn't be sure when, Jacob spun past in a group of four dancers, his face glowing with delight. Liam laughed but Jacob didn't even notice him, and then he was gone again.

Eventually Tamsyn spiralled back into view and taking hold of both of Liam's hands, swung him around and around at arm's length. At the end of one of the rotations she pulled him in and moved her lips close to his ear. The music was thumping and the rhythm of the dancing shook through his body. "Kerenza tells me you're sad that you will forget us."

It hit like a punch to the stomach, he was going to lose it, lose it all. Since arriving at The Sky, Liam had been living utterly in the moment; there was no past, no future, only the eternal now. How could he have forgotten? And yet, wasn't that exactly what he'd wanted? To forget so he could enjoy this last night of bliss. For the second time that evening cruel reality surged over him; a numbing, cold-water shock. And all around the music was driving, pounding, building to an incredible crescendo.

"You really are a dumbass," said Tamsyn, leaning in even closer. Her breath was soft against his ear. Her perfume made his head spin. He could feel the warmth of her body close to his. "You're not going to forget." she whispered.

Then she kissed him, once, a soft brushing of her lips across his cheek. It was the simplest most natural thing, and it blew him away. Then, once again, Tamsyn was lost to him in the chaos of the dance.

EPILOGUE

The tapping on the front door was a surprise; visitors weren't common at the house anymore. At first the man chose to ignore it and remained in his chair, hoping that whomever it was would assume that no one was home and go away again.

Rain rattled against the sitting room window. Surely that would be enough to dissuade them, wouldn't it? But the knocking continued, if anything, becoming more insistent. After a moment or two it was accompanied by a voice calling through the letterbox. The words were indistinct, muffled by two closed doors.

The man sighed and pressed his hands down into the arms of his worn old chair, pushing himself up into a standing position. An involuntary groan escaped his lips and he tutted in irritation. When had an act as simple as standing up become this difficult? The man felt that he was as able and active as he had ever been, but there always seemed to be some new ailment just waiting for an unguarded moment of complacence to remind him of his mortality.

It was easier once he was up and moving - perhaps he wasn't such an old coot after all. Leaving the sitting room behind, the man made his way out into the hall.

The knocking hadn't abated, and he was now able to see an indistinct shadow blocking what little light penetrated the small pane of grimy glass in the front door. A cupped hand was pressed to the window, shading the visitor's eyes as he leaned close to the glass and tried to peer in.

The absence of guests and the man's general disinterest in anything at all over the last few years had allowed the house to age with him. If he answered the door, the person waiting on the other side was going to see how neglected it had become.

He looked despondently around at the dull walls. The passing years seemed to have sucked the light and colour out of them, just as they were doing to him. Tattered cobwebs, only good for trapping dust, hung in the upper corners of the room, wafting in the sluggish air currents. Even the spiders seemed to have left.

A rivulet of water ran down the rain spattered glass as the man peered through. The figure outside had turned away again, dark-coated and shrug-shouldered, enduring the rain. Even though he was facing the road, there was something instantly familiar about him; something in the way he stood and his choice of clothes. The man hadn't seen that hat before, but he knew who'd love it. The subtle bouncing on his toes, the general inability to stand still, the angle of his head; those things hadn't changed.

Quickly, the man fumbled with the door lock and freed the security chain. Any concerns he had about how the place looked were forgotten. If he took too long opening the door the moment would pass and the visitor might leave. Hearing the noise, the visitor turned back to face the house. The door swung inward and there was that smile.

"Hello Dad," said Jacob.

Peter Trevorrow stood in his doorway staring out through the rain at his son. "Jacob," he said.

Jacob swatted rainwater from his brow. "Can I come in? It's a bit wet out here."

A fine dew of water coated his black beanie hat, touching each fibre with the silver of dawn cobwebs. Where his hair poked out it hung in clumps; heavy and wet. "Yes, yes, of course you can. Come in. Come in." Peter flung the door back so quickly that it banged against the wall and he had to catch hold of it to stop it swinging closed again.

In the kitchen, it turned out that the son he last remembered as an orange juice drinker now seemed to be a registered caffeine addict. After pouring boiling water over two heaped teaspoonfuls of cheap, gritty instant coffee and an equal amount of sugar, Peter handed the mug to Jacob. How anyone could drink coffee that strong was a mystery.

Peter led his son into the dingy sitting room. offering him a chair and dropping heavily into his own. "Look, Jacob..." he began.

"No, Dad, please - let me speak first. You've tried loads of times over the years to try and explain to me why you and Mum split up, but I didn't want to know. All I wanted to do was blame you for it. I need to apologise."

Peter blinked away confusion and tears. This was all wrong. His estranged son was back, and somehow was actually apologising to him - apologising to the man who had split up their family, who had caused his own son to suffer ridicule at school. Peter Trevorrow was humbled.

Now that Jacob was back, the old desperation to share everything he knew about Lyskerrys surfaced again. After all, who wouldn't want to tell their only son of a discovery as exciting, as life changing, as utterly thrilling as a gateway to another world. A world where magic was real, and the night sky was alive.

But that path would lead to the same place it had done all those years ago: ridicule, pain, and loss.

And then there was that stupid, stupid plan - stealing the Soul of Lyskerrys and bringing it back here - what on earth had he been thinking? It was only supposed to be for a little while, a misguided attempt to repair the damage that his discovery had caused. The way time was between here and Enys Avalen, they wouldn't even miss it. And then, Jacob would have to believe him, and not just believe, Jacob would share in the joy Peter had found in Lyskerrys.

Of course, it hadn't turned out that way. For some reason the Soul didn't make it back, and Peter had returned to Liskeard empty handed. He had lost the Soul. It had been a stupid idea for sure, but he never meant to lose the Soul. What would happen to Lyskerrys without it? Of course, he could never return. How would they treat the person who had stolen the Soul of Lyskerrys? How could he ever explain it to them? How could they ever forgive the foolish architect of their destruction? And if he could never go back, he could never share it with his son.

"Jacob, I..." began Peter, the words catching in his throat. After all he'd done, did he still have the right to embrace his own son?

Jacob answered his question for him, pulling him into a hug.

In that instant, Peter was transported back to the maternity ward twenty odd years ago when the nurse had first handed him his new-born son. He had been terrified then that he was not holding him correctly. Was that really over twenty years ago? It could have been yesterday.

"I met a girl," said Jacob. "Daisy, from work. She's nice - you'd like her."

"Yeah? That's good," said Peter softly. To speak any more loudly would cause his voice to break. Why would Jacob want to share this important detail of his life with him, after all he had done? How many of these precious moments had he missed over the years thanks to his foolish obsession?

"Yeah, well, we haven't been seeing each other long, but... you know."

Peter's voice wavered. "Listen Jacob, all that stuff, you don't need to apologise. None of it was your fault. You were just a child. I was supposed to be the parent. I should have seen the damage I was doing but I was too wrapped up in my own stupid obsession with the Otherworld to think about the effect it was having on you. I was a fool, that place was all I could think of. I thought I could fix things. It's over now, Lyskerrys, I mean. It's gone, you won't have to hear about it anymore."

"Yeah," said Jacob, slowly, "about that..."

ABOUT THE AUTHOR

Robert has been living in a fantasy world for as long as he can remember. It's entirely possible it all started at an English boarding school in the late 1970s. It's no secret that those places are hubs of magical activity with strong links to other realities, and that kind of thing can leave a lasting impression on a chap.

His stories really started to develop when his sons came along. During their early years, normality was often interrupted by a band of invisible pirates on a mission to disrupt Christmas. These interludes inevitably began with the arrival of a story on their doorstep, which would trigger a chase around the local countryside looking for clues. Those original stories were the catalyst that led to Robert's first novel: The Solstice Blade.

Never comfortable with writing about himself in the third person, he still finds himself doing so when composing the About the Author sections for his books. It is a habit he intends to dispense with by the next paragraph.

There, I told you I'd stop with that nonsense. Having hopefully already thanked everyone I need to in the acknowledgments section, all that remains is to thank you for taking the time to read The Soul of Lyskerrys. It really is appreciated. If all went according to plan then you will have enjoyed a break from reality in a world that may not exist, but really, really should. If you enjoyed your time in Enys Avalen, then I am a happy man. And if you feel inclined, then a short review (or longer if you like) on Amazon and/or Goodreads would be most welcome and help to raise the profile of The Soul of Lyskerrys in this world.